H. M. McNutt

The Old Treasurer

A Three-Act Drama

H. M. McNutt

The Old Treasurer
A Three-Act Drama

ISBN/EAN: 9783337342784

Printed in Europe, USA, Canada, Australia, Japan

Cover: Foto ©Andreas Hilbeck / pixelio.de

More available books at **www.hansebooks.com**

THE

OLD TREASURER

A

THREE-ACT DRAMA,

BY

H. M. McNutt.

PUBLISHED BY

Bessemer Printing & Publishing Company,

Bessemer, Ala.

1893.

DRAMATIS PERSONÆ.

Philip Breen...................................

Rev. Calvin Brockway..........................

Dr. Matthew Zimmerman.......................

Capt. Alex Nelson.............................

Stephen Venable ....

Tandy Trip....................................

Uncle Reuben.................................

Mr. Buck.....................................

Capt. Cole....................................

Ned Boyer....................................

Jack Goozle...................................

First Gambler.................................

Second Gambler..... ....

Third Gambler................................

Martha Delmar...............................

Aunt Martha Holloway........................

Rachel Buck..................................

Glenn McNair................................

Mary Gary.... ›.............................

THE OLD TREASURER.

ACT 1st.

SCENE—*A Southern City on the Coast   Buck's Inn.   The Office.   An old fashioned high desk on L. window on L. with curtains.   Stairway on R.   Large door at back center leading out on long porch.   Long table at Center of stage.   Rachel Buck seated at desk on high stool writing.*

Rachel. (*Tearing up paper.*) Pshaw! I've a good notion not to write to him at all. Now what imp of the old scratch made him say so much about his "Pretty Cousin Donnie?" And I was so happy, too. O, My! but he is so sweet. (*Kissing everything in sight.*) "Cousin Donnie!" (*Slamming everything.*) "And with eyes like those of a young fawn." Dear me! how poetic he was! "Young fawn"—dog's foot! As pretty as those of a young puppy! I won't stand it! I won't! I will show him how to talk about his pretty cousin's eyes. I don't believe she's got any eyes. I wish she was a puppy, I'd drown her mighty quick. I'll show him what I can do. (*Writes furiously.*) "Mr. Withers: I see you have given your heart to another. Please consider yourself released from our engagement.

Respectfully,
RACHEL BUCK."

Now, where are my envelopes? They are all gone. Well, here's a business envelope and this is business. "If not delivered in ten days return to Buck's Inn." (*She seals it but fails to address it.*) Now it will get to Trenton almost as soon as he will.

(*Enter* UNCLE REUBEN *with a load of kindling wood in his arms which he throws into box by fireplace on L.*

Ah! Uncle Reuben, you are just in time. Here's a letter I want you to mail for me. And don't let any one see it. Hear?

Uncle R. Gway fum heah, chile, whut you talkin' about? Aint I done fotch your letters to dat white yankee eber week sence last Christmas? (*Puts letter in his hat.*)

Rach. By the way, Uncle Reuben, here's a letter for you.

Uncle R. Is day? De lawsy me! Miss Rachel, honey,—read it fo' me.

Rach. Yes, and it's from Shubuta.

Reuben. De lawsy me! Dat makes me hongry eber time I hears dat word. Open it, honey, open it.

Rachel. She answers promptly. It was only last Sunday that you wrote to her accusing her of forsaking you. (*Aside.*)—Evidently written by some white person.

"Dear Mr. Watson: (*He grins.*)

I must confess that I was very much surprised by the tenor of your letter—"

Uncle R. De which?

Rach l. That means at the way in which you wrote. "You accuse me of being forgetful and untrue to you, ank you say that I have forsaken you. It is so far from the truth that it requires only a few words to controvert it entirely." Why, Uncle Reuben! (*He laughs and chuckles, striking his knee with his hand.*) "You left here last New Year's Eve, promising to write to me and you didn't keep your promise. I waited and waited and then wrote to you. But you didn't answer. I waited and watched for your answer until I was almost sick, but no letter came. Now, ten months after, you write that *I* have forsaken *you*. No, Mr. Watson, you are like all the men on earth, charming—" Uncle Reuben, are you charming?

Uncle R. Decd I is, honey! Deed I is! Aint I been married six times?

Rachel. Well, Uncle Reuben. You didn't tell me the truth about this case between you and "Miss" Angeline Oakley.

Uncle R. I knows I diden, honey, but whut diffuns does dat make wid Angeline way up at Shubootay and me way down here?

Rachel. Now this alters the case entirely. Your Queen is still true to you and you just sit right down and write to her that you are standing here at your cabin thieshold with your arms outstretched ready to receive her.

Uncle R. Oh, no, Honey, dat wont do, dat wont do.

Rachel. Why?

Uncle R. Caze she mought come sho' nuff.

Rachel Ha! Ha! Ha! You old Antediluvian coquet! You ought to be ashamed.

Reuben. (*Much hurt.*) Now, Miss Rachel. You calls me sich a word as dat, *Me*, old Reuben, what youster tote your Maw in my arms when she was a leetle baby? And look at dat, chile. Look at dat bunt place dar *on* my arm and on my nake. You knows what made it.

Rachel. Yes, Yes, Uncle—

Reuben. *You* knows. You done heard it before.

Rachel. (*Aside.*) Forty times, at least.

Uncle R. Your Maw was runnin' roun whar we was skallin' hogs and laughin' so puddy and lookin' so sweet. She was de puddiest chile. She was de puddiest chile, fer a *white* chile, dat eber I did see; and fust ting I knowd she was slippin' rite into de troff of hot bilin' water. En I seed her just in time to jump and pull her away from de ve age of de water, en den I fell en mer sef. I didn't stay dar long dough, No sirree. If eber a nigger did move, I was dat nigger. I jist tought my whole complexion was done gone. And I diden know nuffin atter dat, till bymeby I wuk up and I tought your Maw be bunt to death, and I jist cried and cried and cried: and when dey told me she wurn't hurt a bit, I say, says I. "Bless de Lam!" En, Honey, I aint felt so happy fum dat day to dis. En now Miss Sarah's baby is done riz up and call me sich a word as dat.

Rachel. What word?

Uncle R. You knows what word well ernuff.

Rachel. When?

Uncle R. You knows when well nuff, too.

Rachel. Where?

Uncle R. Whar? Whut's de matter wid you, white chile? Whar? Wy, right heah. Whar else is I ben?

Rachel. Why, Uncle Reuben, what's the matter with you? You must have been conjured. I have just come in the office.

Uncle R. But can't you onderstan nothin'? Whar's your gumtion gone to anyways? Arter you done red this letter to me—

Rachel. What letter?

Uncle Reuben. Wy, dis letter right here. Can't you see it in my han'?

Rachel. Why, Uncle Reuben, have you received a letter? Let me see it.

Uncle R. Look heah, white chile, Look heah. Tell me dis. (*She looks at him with eyes stretching wider and wider feigning insanity.*) Wusn't you at dat desk writin' when I come in wid de wood and diden you say dar wus a letter fer me and diden— Whut makes you look at me dat way fur?

Rachel. (*In hoarse whisper*) I'm in a trance. I can see clear through your heart. I know what you've been doing.

Uncle R. Lord, Honey, please don't hyst your eyes day, way. I haint done nuffin to nobody.

Rachel. Didn't you see me last Sunday night in the shape of a big black sow with one ear—

Uncle R. Ugh!

Rachel. Cut off, just a runnin' up and down the side of your cabin without makin' any noise?

Uncle R Lawsy me! Honey, How did you know' dat?

Rachel. I tell you I can see clean through you. I know everything you ever did. Hold still. There! There sits Kalline in your heart.

Uncle R. But, Honey—

Rachel. What's that? Skeletons of chickens, roosters, hens and pullets

Uncle R. (*On his knees*) Please, Honey, please don't do dat. Please come to your sef, and let your eyes down and I'll do anything fer yer—anything in Gaw-dlemighty's world.

Rachel. Go, mail my letter.

Uncle R. Yes'm. (*Exit hastily.*)

Rachel. Ha! Ha! Ha! (*Laughing immoderately as Martha enters.*)

Martha. Ha! Ha! Why, Rachel, what on earth have you done to Uncle Reuben? He passed me as I was coming up out of the flower pit, gave a little whoop and away he went. Is he crazy?

Rachel. Why, Ha! Ha! Ha! I told him— Ha! Ha! Ha!

Martha. You've been imposing on his ignorance again, I warrant. And I have been watching a snake eating a mocking bird.

Rachel. A what?

Martha. A snake.

Rachel. What mocking bird?

Martha. What mocking bird! Do you suppose I know them all by name?

Rachel. It can't be mine, surely. (*Exit on porch hastily.*)

Martha. Ha! Ha! Ha! Oh, it was beautiful! Now, she'll cry. By the way, I wonder if the mail has come. Why, yes. Here's a letter from Nell Hodge. I don't care anything for that. I don't like women anyway. She promised to send me a paper with description of our commencement exercises. Pshaw! Wonder why she— Here it is! Here it is! "Thirty-Second Congress" "Four hundred mules for sale." "Horrible Holocaust in Madrid." "Run away with his own wife." What a fool! "Larry's Liver Pills." "The Beautiful Greek." "Scratched 19 Years." "American Atheneum"—Oh! that's it! "Last night the spacious halls of the American Atheneum for young ladies—" Let's see. Let's see. Ah! Miss Martha Siddins Delmar— Siddins! S-I-D-D-I-N-S! The calf. Just like an idiotic reporter. "Was radiant with pearls, diamonds and old lace." Of course she was. So was Noah's wife at her commencement. And the newspaper reporter said just the same thing of her. "Shining like a new-made planet stood forth the fine dramatic work of Miss Martha Delmar in her recitation. She stood and moved with all the bearing and dignity of a Queen, and the words leaped forth from her throat upon a voice at once strong, musical, clear and, at times, strangely pathetic. Then again it was overwhelming While it can be truthfully said that all the ladies evinced marked talent and thorough training, the work of Miss Delmar was nothing less than genius! Genius of the rarest type!" And with an exclamation point, too. These are good critics, these reporters. Ah! Here's my name again. "During the recitation of Miss Delmar, there was a slight disturbance in the audience owing to the sickness of a lady who had fainted." Fainted? Ah! that's power! That's power! And tell me I am not animated by the lineal blood of the great actress? Pshaw! I know it! I feel it! I cannot be separated from it! It possesses my whole life! Everything else and all things earthly are mere pigmies that crawl and grovel at the base. And shall I spend my life in this humdrum place? Among ignorance, superstition, simplicity, soft hearts and empty heads? Bah! (*Striding tragically.*) (*Capt. Nelson is singing without.*) Ah! here comes the first barrier in my way —'the old treasurer"—so-called. Singing his old song, his only song, the full extent of his musical capacity. "The harp that once through Tara's halls, its soul of music shed, now hangs as mute on Tara's walls as if that soul were dead." He's in a good humor then. If anything goes wrong at the Treasury he does'nt sing, but just walks, walks, walks, on his stick and lame leg—

Capt. N. (*Without*) Glenn! Glenn! You rascal, where are you? (*As he enters, Martha, who has hid behind door, slips behind him and places her hands over his eyes.*)

Capt. N. Ah! you little rogue! Glenn! No? It isn't Rachel. Her hands are not so soft. Nor Stephen. His are not so small.

Martha. Ha! Ha! Ha! I fooled the old wizard for once anyway.

Capt. N. Martha! Well. well. The stately, dignified Martha! (*Aside*)—What does she mean? I have never known her to play with me since she was a little child. (*Sits and opens his mail.*)

Martha. How are you, Uncle?

Capt. N. I am well, thank you. And how, are you, Martha ?

Martha. Oh, I'm just as well as I can be. And, look, Uncle, what the paper says about me.

Cap. N. (*Reading it hurriedly*) Yes, Yes, that's nice. That's very neat indeed. Why, I am proud of you, child. I am, indeed. (*Affecting indifference.*) But where's Glenn ?

Martha. She went riding with Philip.

Capt. N. Riding ? Did she ride "Lochinvar?"

Martha. No, sir. She rode "Pluck."

Cap. N. Tut. Tut. Tut. She will persist in riding that horse. He is very treacherous.

Martha. I begged her not to take him, for he looks so vicious; but she would do it. If she is hurt, it will be no fault of mine. (*Aside*)—If she is killed, the old treasurer will die too and the whole estate be mine! Then run, Pluck, run over ditches, fences, walls, trees, and houses !

Capt. N. What is it you are saying, Martha?

Martha. I was hoping that she might not be killed.

Capt. N. (*More nervous.*) Killed? I feel quite sure of that, and yet it is dangerous, I must admit.

Martha. Why, she is perfectly safe, Uncle. She holds a reign as firmly as a ranger.

Capt. N. True. She does, she does.

Martha. And then the horse knows its Glenn, and he won't hurt her !

Capt. N. Ah! Bless her! Everything loves her!

Martha. But tell me, Uncle; what do you think of my genius?

Capt. N. Your genius? who is he?

Martha. He? My genius, my dramatic genius. Don't you see this ?

Capt. N. Yes, Yes. I forgot.

Martha. Is it not something to make a woman faint?

Capt. N. *What* woman?

Martha. Why, *any* woman, Uncle?

Capt. N. Well, that depends. If she's very nervous from indigestion or biliousness or tight-lacing, or small shoes—

Martha. Oh. Uncle, why don't you love me? (*Affecting tears.*)

Capt. N. I do love you, Martha. What do you mean by such strange excitement?

Martha. You take no interest in my greatest achievments, while you applaud the slightest thing that Glenn does and it makes you happy for a week.

Capt. N. Oh, come, come. Sit down by my knee. Now tell me everything you wish to say. I will listen to you and sympathize with you, too.

Martha. Oh Uncle, do you promise that?

Capt. N. Yes.

Martha. Well, dear Uncle, if I tell you what I want to do you must not tell.

Capt. N. Why, Martha, Martha, are you in love?

Martha. Love! Dog's foot! I mean— Ha! Ha! Ha! Not yet, Uncle. But I'll tell you I have determined to adopt the stage.

Capt. N. What stage?

Martha. Why, I mean to be an actress.

Capt. N. Ac— What! An actress? A play actress?

Martha. Yes, sir. Why not?

Capt. N. Why not? Have you lost all pride and reason? An actress? And would you be content with some little role in the first act in which you dust off the furniture and announce the arrival of some painted Duchess or prancing fop of a Marquis? No, No, Martha, don't think of it, don't think of it.

Martha. But what use can I make of my talent here?

Capt N. Make all those happy around you. Very few can do more.

Martha. Pshaw! And keep myself miserable?

Capt. N. Martha, you know I am very old. I cannot reasonably expect many more years of life on earth. At my death, your property and Glenn's will be held in trust by Stephen Venable who will be my successor—

Martha. (*Aside.*) Stephen!

Capt. N. And if you do not wish to squander it, let it remain where it is. It is not very much, but it is sufficient to support you comfortably as long as you live. Will you not promise me, Martha?

Martha. (*Affecting tears.*) It-seems-very cruel, Uncle, but I'll try. (*Aside*)—In Stephen's hands? And Stephen is in *my* hands. I want nothing better. At his death, too.

Glenn. (*Without.*) Uncle Reuben, has Uncle Alex come yet?

Capt. N. That's Glenn! That's Glenn! Ha! Ha! Ha! (*Enter at door, R. C. Glenn and Philip.*)

Capt. N. Come here, you little rascal. Ha! Ha! Ha!
Glenn. In one moment, Uncle.

Rachal. Why Glenn, where did you—
Glenn. (*Stopping her mouth.*) Hush!
Phil. Wont he see your torn dress?
Glenn. Don't you know a man better than that? Ha! Ha!

Capt. N. (*Impatiently*) Why does she hesitate? Glenn!
Glenn. Yes. Uncle. (*She comes and kneels down by him.*)

Capt. N. Didn't I tell you not to ride that horse until Sam Coburn could break him?
Glenn. Now, Now. Now. Pluck is perfectly safe, Uncle. (*Aside*)—In the stable. (*Aloud.*) Oh, he is d'lightful!
Capt. N. Look at me Glenn. Not that way. Close. (*She mischievously places her nose against his.*) Did that horse try to throw you?

Glenn. Not another word shall you speak. (*Kissing him.*) You alarm yourself unnecessarily. (*Kiss*) You see if (*Kiss*) I can't stop your (*Kiss*) dear old mouth—
Phil. (*Kissing him.*) I can! Ha! Ha! Ha!
Cap'. N. Go away, you rascal. Ha! Ha! Ha!
Phil. Come now, Uncle. I'll have Stephen's job to-night. I'll carry you up to your room, so you may prepare for supper. (*Lifting him.*) Stephen is busy among his friends, no doubt. Come, Anchises, I'll be your Aeneas to-night. (*Carrying him out in his arms.*)
Capt. N. Ah, you're a merry boy, Philip, you're a merry boy. Oh, Glenn, you will find a letter there on

the table concerning our new minister which you may
read. *(Exeunt Phil. and Capt. N.)*

Rachel. Tell me, Glenn, where on earth did you
tear your dress so?

(Martha is seated near window behind curtains.)

Glenn. Oh, but you'll tell?

Rachel. What do you take me for?

(Re-enter Philip.)

Phil. By grabs, but that was a close shave.

Glenn. Yes, and it's the second close shave I've had
to-day. For a woman without much beard I think
that's doing pretty well. Ha! Ha! Ha!

Rachel. *(Almost crying)* Well, what is it? What
is it? Do you want me to spontaneously combust
with curiosity?

Phil. Oh, Rachel, we have had such a time of it!

Rachel How?

Glenn. But you won't tell? *(Martha is listening.)*

Rachel *(Offended.)* Well, if you think I hav'nt
sense enough to hold my tongue, you needn't. *(Walking away.)*

Glenn. Oh, if you are angry with me, I think we'd
better not tell you.

Rachel. *(Returning quickly.)* I'm not angry with
you, Glenn; indeed I'm not. I just love you, Glenn.
Who said I was angry? Now, please tell me, Glenn.

Glenn. *(Whispering.)* Pluck ran away with me—

Rachel. Oh!

Glenn. Threw me off—

Rachel. Gracious!

Glenn. Dragged me along the road—

Rachel. Oh, my!

Glenn. Tearing my dress half off and leaving my
arms and shoulders bare—just look at me!—and Philip got down and came to me as pale as a ghost and
looked into my face and I just broke out laughing—
he looked so funny—Ha! Ha! and then he lifted me
up and took off his coat and put it on me—Ha! Ha!
The question then was, what was Philip to do with
out a coat. If Uncle knew I had such a narrow es-
cape, it would almost kill him. So Philip was
afraid to come home without his coat for fear
Uncle, in some way would discover it; so he went
through the old alley back of the jail to the treasurer's

office, raised a window, got out this old coat of Stephen's, put it on and came away.

Rachel. Oh, Glenn, what do you think? Martha wants to go on the stage.

Glenn. The stage! Ha! The stage! "Half past nine and Mr. Charles has not yet arrived," or "Give me back me poverty and me honor." (*Walking romaneiquely and describing a large semi-circle.*) You know it means nothing unless you sweep the whole stage, Rachel.

Rachel. Ladies and gentlemen, I am requested to announce that to-morrow night we will present Shakespeare's sublime tragedy called "Hamlet," or I am thy Father's Ghost!"

Glenn. Don't say "thy father." Say "the father."

Rachel. That ain't the way they do it on the stage.

Glenn. I know. But they'll come to it. They say me father now, you know.

Martha. (*Aside.*) Ah, but, my merry girls, I will see acting as it is in real life, not on the stage. And you are the subjects I'll use in my study as a scientist would experiment with a rat or a dog.

Glenn. By the way, Philip, you'd better go and find Stephen now.

Phil. That's true, I forgot. (*Exit.*)

Rachel. What for?

Glenn. We found the vault doors open.

(*Martha slips out slowly from curtains and goes out unobserved.*)

Glenn. I'll go up now and change my dress. (*Incidentally running her hands in the pockets of the coat.*) Hello, what a pile of old letters. Some of my own, too. Ha! Ha! But the new minister, Rachel, lets read it. (*Holding the letter in her hand.*)

Rachel. All right. (*They go to the light back of the desk and read the letter.*)

Glenn. What's his name, I wonder. (*Enter at the door Dr. Zimmerman and Rev. Calvin Samuel Brockway.*) What's that? Rev. C. S. Brockway.

Calvin. (*To Dr.*) Hello, my name, the first thing.

Doctor. Hush!

Glenn. I wonder what C. S. stands for?

Rachel. Don't know. King Solomon, I reckon.

Glenn. I suppose so. Hello, Sol.; how are your wives?

Doctor. (*To Calvin.*) Hush!

Glenn. Why, this is not a letter of recommendation. Look here. "He engenders so-called progressive ideas which are very pernicious in their effect upon young minds and are really dangerous to any religious community." Pshaw! I venture to say he is a good man.

Calvin. (*To Doctor.*) Just as I expected.

Doctor. The old vampire! I don't believe that nitric acid would have any effect on him. He is rank poison himself.

Glenn. Well, come on, King Solomon, I'll be glad to see you.

Calvin. I believe you will.

Glenn. Oh! Ha! Ha! Ha! (*She and Rachel hide their faces behind the open letter.*)

Rachel. Do you wish to register, gentlemen?

Doctor. If you please. Miss Rachel.

Rachel. Miss Rachel.

Enter MR. BUCK.

Buck. (*To Doctor*) Why, brother, howdy do? Howdy! Howdy! I declare you are looking powerful well. You don't appear to know me.

Doctor. No, sir. I do not. (*Calvin and Doctor register their names.*)

Buck. Why dont you remember the meeting three years ago down at Hollywood church? My son Bob professed religion under you.

Doctor. The devil he did! (*Rachel and Glenn laugh.*)

Buck. Sir? Well—no. I believe I'm mistaken. But you do look powerful like him. (*Exit.*)

Doctor. Your pardon, ladies. The gentleman took me by surprise and my tongue acted independently

Rachel. (*Reading names on register.*) Why, Glenn, this is the new preacher.

Glenn. What? Which one?

Calvin. Ecce homo. King Solomon, as you call him, though the old folks at home call me "Calvin," and this is my guardian and godfather, Dr. Zimmerman.

Glenn. Your Godfather!

Doctor. Yes. His partner in everything except

his faith. I am his doctor, his seamstress, his porter, his washwoman, his protector, his aid-de-camp, his general and his corporal.

Glenn. He looks sufficiently able to protect himself

Doctor. Oh, but he is not, I assure you, and, in doing so—

Glenn. At any rate, I will assist you to protect him myself.

Doctor. You? No, no, no! You are the enemy.

Glenn. I am sure I do not feel so.

Doctor. Then I must swear you both.

Glenn. Swear us?

Doctor. Yes.

Glenn. To what?

Doctor. You are not desperately anxious to marry, are you?

Glenn. To marry? Ha! Ha! Ha! Well, the proposition coming from a stranger is unusually sudden, but—

Calvin. Oh, No! No! No! You don't understand.

Doctor. You see, we came from an old town where there are nothing but old men and females of all ages. We spent the summer at Glade Sulphur Springs and we were the only eligible men there. Now, please, please spare us! (*On their knees.*)

Calvin. In mercy spare us!

Glenn. Oh, we can't think of it, can we Rachel?

Rachel. By no means. Gentlemen, we love you and will make you our husbands, by our halidom. Ha! Ha! Ha!

Glenn. King Solomon, I will protect you, I will be your body-guard. Our much beloved pastor, I extend to you the heartiest welcome a Southern heart can give. May you be the light of every fireside, a sunbeam on every desolate hearthstone, a comfort to every heart, a father to every homeless ragamuffin, and a brother to all mankind.

Calvin. My doctrine exactly. Miss McNair, your words have been a warm and blessed unction to my heart. I thank you, I thank you. (*Warmly taking her hand.*)

Glenn. Dr. Zimmerman, you are welcome to our

beloved country, and to this blessed old inn, where nothing but good cheer ever reigned.

Doctor (*To Calvin.*) I swear old man, she's better than the best old rye I ever drank. By the way, Miss McNair, I see you have torn your dress. If you will just permit me, I will mend it for you. (*Opening his valise for needle and thread.*)

Glenn. You mend my dress?

Calvin. Ha! Ha! Ha! Don't be offended, I pray you. My friend is an altruist run mad. It's mere force of habit I assure you. Why he nursed every baby on the boat, coming down the river and came very near having one left on his hands, too. Sew? Well, you should see him in his room, seated on his table, smoking his pipe and sewing on dresses and little breeches.

Glenn. Dresses? Is he married?

Doctor. No, No! But you see, we always look up those little chaps that have no mother at home. Calvin makes their hearts happy, while I look after their stomachs and bodies. I can patch a pair of pants and cure a stone bruise. I can sew on buttons with one hand and pull a tooth with the other.

Calvin. And he can no more resist the impulse to help anyone in any undertaking than he can fly. Some very sweet pickles, he gets himself into by it, too.

Glenn. A most beautiful fault, nevertheless.

Calvin. Why, if he stood and watched a burglar trying to open his own safe, and making a desperate effort at it, he would say very politely, "I beg your pardon, but I think I can help you."

Glenn. Why, that is splendid.

Calvin. Then you must enjoy such work yourself?

Glenn. I do, more than anything else.

Calvin. Do you know many of the poor people here?

Rachel. Many! Yes, *manier*. Ask her whose baby is teething and what's good for it, how much wood old Mrs. Riggles has laid in for the winter, when little Tim Dreck will be able to sell "sassafrac" again, how much the old basket maker earns, how many children are fed by the parish. Everything that's nobody's business is Glenn McNair's business.

Stephen. (*At the door speaking to Philip.*) Ha! Ha! Ha! But you don't believe such things; do you Philip? (*Tossing up a coin and catching it.*)

Phil. Well, yes. I do.

Stephen. Pshaw! Ha! Ha! Ha!

Glenn. Hurrah for the next mayor of the city. Hurrah!

Calvin. Hurrah!

Glenn. Louder!

Calvin. Hurrah!!

Glenn. That's something like it. (*Enter Aunt Martha and Capt. Alex.*) Now the Mayor doesn't know but that you are a human being and not a sanctimonious poor creature that is afraid he will infect his lungs with the atmosphere of this vile earth. Stephen, what is this? (*Pointing to Calvin.*)

Stephen. Well, at this distance he has all the appearance of the genus homo.

Glenn. Is he a lawyer, or a doctor, or a merchant, or a horse racer, or a gambler, or a circus agent?

Stephen. He might possibly be a combination, but I don't believe it.

Glenn. Mr. Venable, the Rev. Calvin Brockway.

Stephen. What?

(*Enter Martha Siddons.*)

Glenn. And his friend, Dr Zimmerman.

Stephen. Gentlemen, you are right welcome to our home. Gentlemen, allow me to acquaint you with Capt. Nelson, Mrs. Holloway, Miss Delmar, and Mr. Breen.

Doctor. (*To Capt.*) Don't rise, sir, don't rise. We'll come to you.

Capt. N. Thank you, sir. Your hands, gentlemen. You are welcome to the Inn. (*Enter Mary Gary carrying lamps.*) Ah, Mary, good evening.

Mary. Good avening to ye, Capthain, I hope ye air well, Capthain?

Capt. N. Quite well, thank you, Mary. Gentlemen, I have the honor of introducing to you Miss Mary Gary.

Doctor. (*Aside.*) What! The chambermaid? (*Bowing.*)

Mary. Good avening, gentleman. I be glad to mate you.

Doctor. (*Aside*) Introduce us to such cattle as that?

Calvin. (*Laughing in his sleeve at Doctor's surprise.*) It's all right. You are in America, now, my boy.

(*Exit Mary.*)

Capt. N. Gentlemen, I see you do not understand.

Doctor. I beg your pardon Captain, but have you in the South no regard for class distinction? Do you always show such deference to serving people?

Capt. N. No, not always. But this woman is worthy of the lowest bow of the Czar of Russia.

Doctor. Indeed? How? Is she a duchess or Princess in disguise?

Capt. N. Better still. She is a woman, gentlemen, that sat in a chair for three weeks holding in her arms her little namesake niece whose lips the surgeon had sewed for hair lip. The little child must be watched to prevent her tearing the threads asunder, and there Mary sat and watched her charge for three weeks. Then leaving her one day in other hands for a short time, she became fretful and with her restless fingers tore loose the threads. The operation was again performed, and there she sat another three weeks until the little one recovered entirely.

(*Pause.*)

Doctor. (*Scratching his chin.*) Well, now, if I were an ostrich or a boa-constrictor I might digest that story.

Stephen. Oh, it's true, every word of it.

Doctor. Miss Glenn, will you swear to the truth of that hair-lip story?

Glenn. Yes. For I saw her every day and every night.

Doctor. You did? Is it possible? Well, well. May I see her again? She's better than a duchess, Captain, for a duchess wouldn't do it.

Calvin. Most remarkable.

Doctor. Duchess, did I say? She's worthy to sit by the Queen of England and teach her the divine unselfishness of her sex!

Glenn. (*Applauding.*) And you say you're an Englishman?

Doctor. Yes.

Glenn. I don't believe it.

Doctor. Ha! Ha! I see you've lost a leg, Captain. Must I ask your pardon for that?

Capt. N. No, sir. The Mexicans did that.

Doctor Where?

Capt. N. At Buena Vista.

Doctor. I suppose your government recognized your loss in a material way?

Capt N. Oh, yes, sir. They gave me a medal, sir, along with Capt. Davis and several others.

Doctor. And a pension?

Capt. N. No, sir, no pension. They offered one but I would not accept it.

Doctor. Why, may I ask?

Capt. N. Why should I? I returned from the war with one good leg, two good arms and one good head. I said I was able to support myself and I have done it. Besides, I did not fight for money. I fought for my country. Pension. Bah! The State takes care of paupers, criminals and lunatics, and should not be made a vast alms-house for those abundantly able to care for themselves.

Glenn. (*To Calvin.*) He can talk on that subject all night.

Doctor. (*Gazing at Captain in thoughtful admiration.*) Brave old soldier.

Stephen. Yes, and he will talk with an imaginary listener, if he can find no one else.

Capt. N. (*To himself.*) I remember once when my mother was very sick so many years ago it seems as if it were in another age. As her life hung by a thread, every possible noise about the house was muffled and everyone went about on tip-toe, noiselessly. Fearing to disturb her, I took "my shoes from off my feet for the place whereon I stood was holy ground." That was a love akin to that which I feel for my country.

(*Pause.*)

Doctor. And you are the City Treasurer?

Capt. N. Yes, sir.

Doctor. When were you elected?

Capt. N. Fifty years ago.

Doctor. Fifty years!

Capt. N. Yes, sir. And always will be.

Doctor. How?

Capt. N. I believe, sir, that when I die, my spirit will go to the old treasury and hover about it continually.

Glenn. Oh, now, now, Uncle. (*Kissing him.*) Talk of something else. By the way, Mr. Parson, here's another kindred spirit for you. (*Putting arm around Stephen.*) If there's a child in the town that doesn't call him "Stephen" it is one that calls him "Tephen."

Stephen. That's true. Oh, I'm the regular and original "Mrs. Winslow's Soothing Syrup." Ha! Ha! Ha!

Calvin. Good. I will enlist you in my service. And some hot day next summer we'll take a steamer and our little homeless partners and go on a long ocean picnic to Australia.

Glenn. Australia! You don't mean it?

Calvin. Indeed I do. Why not?

Glenn. Do you propose to buy a steamer?

Calvin. Oh, no. But it won't cost very much, and my friend here will pay for it, eh Mattie?

Doctor. (*Swelling.*) Yes, of course. It's a trifle, a mere trifle.

Stephen. Then you are wealthy, I suppose?

Doctor. Your supposition is correct, Mr.—Stephen. I'm what pious and disappointed people call a "bloated bond holder."

(*Enter Philip.*)

Phil. Hello, Rach—any letters for me?

Rachel. No.

Phil. Thank the Lord. Whew! My creditors must have died suddenly. Ha! Ha! I haven't heard from them in two days. If they don't dun me tomorrow, I'll go and see them. I can't endure such neglect and I won't! I have some credit as long as they have any hope of getting their money. Ha! Ha! Ha!

Calvin. (*To Martha.*) Is he really in debt?

Martha. Yes, and has been for many years. I have offered to lend him the money but he refuses it.

Stephen What? Exchange his creditors for a woman creditor? and have them come to him. "Oh, Mr. Breen, if you only knew how I have suffered, what agony, what fears, what ills, what privations, what tears I have shed—"

Phil. Stephen, for the Lord's sake, don't teach them that lesson. Don't do it. I'd turn my whole estate over to them if they sent women's tears after me.

Stephen. Ha! Ha! And do you know what he calls his whole estate! One pine trunk, one wedding trousseau as he calls it, a mass of romantic manuscript, and a lot of bric-a-brac carved with his own knife in hours of dreamful meditation. Total value $2.85.

Phil. Correct to the fraction. Stephen, you're a mathematical prodigy. But you have taken no inventory of my gold, silver and diamonds.

Calvin. What does he mean?

Glenn. Listen.

Phil. A wealth of uncoined gold as pure as ever played with a sunbeam nestles in my Susan's tresses!

Doctor and Calvin. Oh!

Phil. Diamonds of such lustre as the Kohinoor never knew sparkle in her eyes.

Doctor. Is it possible?

Phil. Possible? Sir, do you doubt my veracity? Possible! It's a fact.

Stephen. Yes, it is. And the best of it is that his Susan has been married to another man these sixteen years. Ha! Ha!

Calvin. And he still visits her?

Stephen. Hasn't seen her since she married! So you see how long his ears are now, don't you?

Calvin. And you still love her?

Phil. Love her, man! I love her old last year's shoe strings.

Calvin. Pardon my impudence, you take everything so good humoredly.

Phil. Go on, Parson, go on. I'm about as invulnerable as an alligator. There was a time when I watched with chary eyes at the doors of this good temple which I call my heart. Now, it is a venerable ruin under whose shade the weary traveler in the desert of love may rest and receive what comfort he may. Ha! Ha! You see, it has made a poet of me, too.

Calvin. I like, you, Mr Philip, in spite of your poetry. Upon my soul, Miss Delmar, I never saw so many generous and lovely folks. Are all the Southern people like you?

Martha. No, not all. (*Aside.*) Like me, indeed.

Stephen. Parson, listen. Do you hear that?

Calvin. Yes, what is it?

Stephen. Listen. Don't you know?

Doctor. It's a pig under a gate.

Stephen. No.

Doctor. Then it's some poor little Absolom on his mamma's knee responding to the action of the back of a hair brush.

Stephen. No.

Doctor. Then it's a young woman singing.

Stephen. Ha! Ha! More musical than that! It's what Uncle Reuben, our old negro porter, calls a "Squinch owl."

Calvin. An owl?

Stephen. Yes. And I'll tell you what I'll do.

Calvin. What?

Stephen. I'll pledge you anything you may ask of me if old Reuben is not at this very moment heating a poker.

Calvin. For what?

Stephen. To—well I'll call him and let him answer. I venture to say—why, here he is now.

(*Enter Reuben.*)

Reuben. Good even', Mars Stephen.

Stephen. Good evening, Uncle Reuben. What will you have?

Reuben. I jist wants to stir the fire a leetle, sah. Dat's all, sah.

(*They all watch him.*)

Stephen. (*As Reuben is about to go out.*) Oh, Uncle Reuben.

Reuben. Yes, sah.

Stephen. You left the poker in the fire.

Reuben. Yes, sah, if you please sah. I'll take it out, sah, soon as dat squinch owl stop squinching, sah.

Calvin. Are you going to knock the owl in the head with it, Uncle Reuben?

Reuben. No, sah; taint no needcessity fo' dat, sah. Hittle stop when de poker gits hot, sah.

Calvin. Why.

Reuben. I can't tell you dat, sah. Hear dat?

Hear dat silence out dar? I knowd it, sah, I knowd it. (*Takes out poker and puts it in rack.*)

Doctor. Ha! Ha! Ha! And you think the poker stopped him, do you ?

Reuben. Yes, sah, I knows it sah.

(*Exit Reuben.*)

Stephen. Now, you laugh at the superstition of this old negro, what do you think of a full-blooded Caucasian, a proud American, familiar with the Odyssey, the odes of Horace, Pliny; knows the race-course of every star and its name—what do you think when he, Philip Breen, believes in such things?

Doctor. Indeed ?

Calvin. The doctor here has often laughed at me because I have my superstitions, while he by nature is skeptical and scarcely believes anything.

Phil. You laugh at me, Stephen; and yet you have the greatest faith in your good luck—a thing just as vague and uncertain.

Stephen. It is not uncertain at all It is as certain as anything can be. I don't understand it, but I can see it and everyone else can see it, and there's no denying it.

Doctor. What do you mean?

Stephen. My luck at anything that depends on chance. Toss up a coin. Heads or tails?

Doctor. What do you mean by heads or tails?

Stephen. This side is heads and this tails. Toss it up. (*Doctor tosses.*) Heads!

Doctor. Correct. (*Tosses.*)

Stephen. Heads.

Doctor. Correct. (*Tosses several times.*) Stuff. There's some trick in it

Stephen. Not a particle. Try me on something else.

Doctor. And do you mean to say that you believe that chance or fortune is always on your side?

Stephen. Yes.

Doctor. Then you are the most unlucky man I ever saw.

Stephen. Why? (*Aside.*) What does he mean.

Phil. Well, I had a very strange dream last night. You may laugh, Stephen, but I'll tell it.

Stephen. Now, as little Trim Morris says: "Oh,

pease don't, you skeah me moas ter def." Ha! Ha!
Ha!

Phil. I seldom dream as I am very busy when I'm
sleeping.

(*Enter Tandy Tripp and sits on low stool near door.*)

Stephen. Yes, sawing gourds. As Uncle Reuben
would say, your silence is very loud,

Phil. Well, the other night—last Saturday night,
I remember—I dreamt that I met *you*, Martha, on the
street and I never saw you look so strangely before—
it surprised me that I recognized you at all—and you
told me the City Treasury had been robbed and the
Midland Bonds taken therefrom. I seemed then to
understand, but if there are now, or ever were, or ever
will be, any such thing as Midland Bonds in the
treasury I know nothing of it.

Capt. N. You mean to say you never heard of the
Midland bonds?

Phil. Never did, sir. What do I know about
bonds? I don't know whether they are made of steel
or copper or brass or wood. Why, Uncle Alex?

Capt. N. There are $40,000.00 of them there.

Stephen. (*Aside*) I have'nt felt easy about that
vault since I found it open. I'll go and examine it.

Capt. N. Where are you going Stephen?

Stephen. I am going down town for some cigars,
Uncle, I'll be back—

Capt. N. Well— Stephen!

Stephen. Yes, sir.

Capt. N. Come here, please. Stop at the treasury
and examine it, will you?

Stephen. Ha! Ha! Ha! All right, Uncle, I will.
(*Going.*) Why here is Tandy! Hello, Tandy. Glad
to see you.

Tandy. Tanky, sir, Tanky, sir. (*He walks with
head much on one side, talks with many jerks and facial
contortions almost as if from St. Vitus' dance.*)

Glenn. How are you, Tandy?

Tandy. Haw! Haw! I be well, missie, I be well.
I don't want to sell nuffin tonight. I am like Cap'n
Nelson. I don't transact any business after office
hours. Haw! Haw! I just came in to hear the folks
talk. Mr. Buck said I wouldn't be in the way.

Buck. To be sure, to be sure.

Calvin. (*To Martha.*) Who is he?

Martha. An old paralytic. Has been about here several months selling cheap jewelry. (*Aside.*)—I don't know why they allow such an old scare-crow to come in the house.

Calvin. (*Aside.*) She thought I didn't hear her. That is the first unhospitable word I have heard since I came. (*To Captain N.*)—May I converse with this Mr. Tripp, Captain?

Capt. N. Certainly, sir. (*Exit and walks to and fro on porch.*)

Calvin. Mr. Tripp?

Tandy. Haw! Haw! Haw!

Calvin. Why are you laughing so?

Tandy. *Mr. Tripp!* Haw! Haw! Haw!

Glenn. (*To Calvin.*) Call him "Tandy."

Calvin. Tandy?

Tandy. Ay, Ay, Sir.

Calvin. How long have you been so afflicted?

Tandy. Since I was three weeks old, sir.

Calvin. Three weeks old?

Tandy. Yes, sir.

Calvin. Well, you have a pretty good time, don't you?

Tandy. Yes, sir. You see I haint never knowd anything else, sir. Haw! Haw! Haw!

Calvin. Have you had supper tonight?

Tandy. Oh, yes, sir.

Calvin. And you have enough for breakfast?

Tandy. No, sir.

Calvin. What will you do, then?

Tandy. Well, I done had a good supper, haint I?

Doctor. And the prospect for breakfast is too remote for speculation. And you sleep well, Tandy?

Tandy. Oh, yes, sir. I sleep mighty well.

Doctor. Where do you sleep?

Tandy. Where? Haw! Haw! I've got the whole State of Louisiany to sleep on. Haw! Haw!

Doctor. I never knew before what a beautiful leg I have, Calvin. And such an arm, too! You sleep on the ground?

Tandy. Oh, yes, sir. Old Miss Jackson give me a feather bed onct, but it was so soft I could not sleep on it.

Doctor. Where did you sleep last night, Tandy?

Tandy. Under the woodshed at the Cap'ns office, sir.

Calvin. And you are happy, Tandy?

Tandy. Oh, yes, sir. I reckon so, sir.

Calvin. Wouldn't you like to be well and strong?

Tandy. I reckon so, sir. You see, sir, I done been this way so long I wouldn't know what to do if I had good use of myself, sir.

Doctor. You could preach, couldn't you?

Tandy. Oh, yes, sir. I could preach. Haw! Haw!

Calvin. You would make a better doctor than a preacher, wouldn't you?

Tandy. Oh, yes, sir. Any fool can be a doctor. Haw! Haw! Most folks will take eberting te doctor gives 'em anyway.

Calvin. How long do you expect to live, Tandy?

Tandy. I can't tell you nothin' bout that, sir.

Doctor. Are you a member of the church?

Tandy. No, sir.

Doctor. Why?

Tandy. Well, you see, sir, nobody wants me to sit by 'em in church, sir. I tried it several times and they looked around at me jist so. (*Frowns and looks indignant.*) Except once, sir. I went into a church and the young folks begun to laugh and punch each other and hide their faces, jest so. (*Imitating them.*) Nobody would make room for me till at last an old man got up out of his seat, opened te door, tat little door at te end, you know, sir, and bowed to me and waved me in just like tat, and let me look on te same book with him. I don't say who it was, but he had a wooden leg and a walkin' stick I hears it now. Haw! Haw! (*Enter Capt. N.*)

Glenn. (*Kissing him.*) Are you well tonight, Uncle?

Capt. N. I am well, but just a little nervous, my girl. (*Sits.*)

Glenn. (*Aside.*) His eye balls are larger than usual. What does it mean?

Calvin. Tandy, do you wish to die?

Tandy. No, sir. I don't want to die.

Calvin. You believe the Great Father loves you, don't you?

Tandy. I don't know about tat, sir. I used to have a looking glass oncet and lowed then tat I was too onery looking for anybody to love much. Haw! Haw!

Doctor. Do you believe you would go to Heaven?

Tandy. Well, they mought let me slip in and crawl under the throne and go to sleep. Don't you think so?

Calvin. I don't doubt it, Tandy, I don't doubt it.

Tandy. It would be better than the woodshed, too. Nobody would tread on me there as they did tonight; but it didn't hurt, missie, it didn't hurt a bit. (*Glenn and Philip motion him to silence but he doesn't understand.*) It didn't. (*To Phillip.*)—I seen you when you got outer te window, sir. Haw! Haw! (*Enter Stephen quickly.*)

Capt. N. What's the matter, Stephen? (*Very nervously.*)

Stephen. I've been running, Uncle. It's raining.

Capt. N. Raining! Tell me, Stephen. Are those bonds missing?

Stephen. (*Slowly.*) Yes, Uncle.

Capt. N. Great God! (*Sits back in his chair and dies sitting bolt upright with eyes open.*)

Glenn. But they can find them again, Uncle. Don't worry. Uncle, don't— Ha! (*Staggering back on floor.*)

Stephen. What's the matter, Glenn?

Doctor. (*Taking Captain's hand.*) He's dead!

Tandy. (*Coming forward and weeping bitterly.*) I beg your pawden, missie, I beg your pawden. (*Kissing her shoe.*)

Stephen. (*Looking mysteriously about.*) Who is that walking on the gallery?

Phil. Walking? I hear no one walking.

Stephen. You do not hear that walking?

Phil. No.

Stephen. You hear it, don't you, Doctor?

Doctor. What do you mean, man? (*Stephen goes on tiptoe to door, looks out and returns.*)

Stephen. There is no one there, and yet I hear some one walking as with a lame leg and walking-stick.

Phil. Why, Stephen, what's the matter?

Stephen. Philip, do those eyes appear to look at you?

Phil. What eyes?

Stephen. Come here with me. Do they look at you now?

Phil. Are you sick, Stephen?

Stephen. I-do-not-know.

Martha. (*Without.*) Ha! Ha! Ha!

Phillip. (*Placing his hand over her mouth as she enters.*) Hush! (*Martha stands horrified.*)

CURTAIN.

ACT 2d.

Scene.—*Same as Act 1st.*

(*Enter Aunt Martha, Mary Gary and Rachel the last bustling about and slamming everything as she goes.*)

Rachel. (*To Aunt Martha.*) You hope she'll be convicted. I know *you* do. I always thought you were one of those crocodile Christians!

Aunt Martha. You naughty girl! I hope Glenn may not be convicted, but it all comes upon her for neglecting her church, and I was always afraid she'd never come to any good.

Rachel. Yes, and because—

Mary. And it ain't thot oid be disagraing wid ye, Misthress Marthy, but ye don't appair to be happy, Misthress Marthy, unliss you can foind some one thet's goin' to Purgatory, Misthress Marthy, so ye can give 'em a kick, Misthress Marthy.

Aunt Martha. What? You dare argue with me? (*Aside.*) This comes of having these hateful white servants.

Mary. Why don't ye spake out so a body can hear ye? And as for Miss Glenn and Mr. Philip, your long confissions never made anything half as good, Misthress Marthy. They wouldn' hesertate to take you into their big warrum hearts, Misthress Marthy, if ye were the manest of all mankind—which the same ye air Misthress Marthy.

Aunt Martha. I'm sure many's the tears I've shed over her. I've begged and implored her to go with me to the meetings, to the Ladies' Aid, to the Gospel Readings, but she would only laugh at me. Now, see what's come upon her.

Rachel. She does go to church, And she does many other things that are better than your long-faced prayer meetings. She is helping somebody in their troubles while you are folding your hands and looking as pious as a tombstone.

Aunt Martha. Oh, you wicked lost spirit! You call it nothing? What time have I for such things as she and that new-fangled, worldly preacher are doing. He won't stay here three months either, I warrant. For when my boy Richmond returns from the Southern Presbyterian College he'll show him how to respect the holy calling.

Rachel. Your son Richmond can show him the "Royal Flush" too.

Aunt Martha. And there's your brother Bobby. Poor boy! I don't know what he'd do if I didn't mend his morals occasionally.

Rachel. (*Imitating.*) Poor boy! I don't know what he'd do if I didn't mend his breeches occasionally. Look here, Aunt Martha, what Buck's Inn needs is less worship and more work. You understand? You are always piling up treasures in heaven and at the same time you eat the treasures we pile up on earth.

Aunt Martha. Why, child, I arose yesterday morning at 6 o'clock and read seven chapters in Numbers before breakfast.

Rachel. Did you cook breakfast? No. At six! I was up at five and fed the chickens and the pigs, churned the milk, waited on the table, made some catnip tea for Mrs. Gaunt's baby, washed the dishes, made three little dresses for Stephen's "little partners," helped to cook dinner, helped Uncle Reuben to hive a swarm of bees, got the gun and shot a hawk—

Aunt Martha. Oh, the horrid thing! It frightened me dreadfully!

Rachel. Drove the pigs out of the garden, took a music lesson, hung up the clothes to dry, turned the grindstone for Uncle Reuben, fed a tramp for carrying

them old rocks away from the back door which he
promised to do and didn't—

Aunt Martha. Served you right. Why do you—

Rachel. Oh, but I gave him such a larrupin' with
the buggy whip as will compel him to stand hereafter
when engaged in eating his food.

Aunt Martha What a spit-fire she is! Oh, child
if your poor dear mother, could only—

Rachel. My poor dear mother was as different from
you as I am. She was the best woman that ever
lived, if she *was* a Presbyterian. You are nothing
but a Presbyterian.

Aunt Martha. Yes, I am a Presbyterian. And
that young preacher you've brought here is no more
a Presbyterian than a circus-clown. (*Enter Tandy
Tripp.*) Why, he has even got that vagabond, Tandy
Tripp to going to church and sitting up in the very
best pews—

Mary. "And aven the poor," Misthress Marthy,
"have the Gospel preached unto them," Misthress
Marthy.

Aunt Martha. Oh, Mary, you are one of these
Catholics. The Roman Catholics would let the very
Evil one into heaven.

Mary. Yes, Oi *am* a Catholic! Misthress Marthy, and we would let the divil in if it would make
a better man of him, Misthress Marthy, and it moight
be more comfortabler for ye, Misthress Marthy, if we
could do it, Misthress Marthy; ye have no more hu-
manity in your bones than an Egyptian mermaid.
Misthress Marthy. You don't love nobody and nobody loves you, Misthress Marthy.

Aunt Martha. You shut your mouth, Mary Gary.
What do you know about my love affairs?

Rachel. Her love affairs! Ha! Ha! Ha!

Aunt Martha. You laugh at me, you insulting creatures? I will not contaminate myself longer by your
society. I can scarcely breathe! (*Exit, holding her
nose.*)

Rachel. Ha! Ha! Mary, we deprive her of her
oxygen! Ha! Ha! Ha!

Mary. Contaminate, is it? Oi'll contaminate her
wid a froyin' pan if she makes fun of me church agin,
I will.

Rachel. Why, there is Tandy. When did you come, Tandy?

Tandy. I benn here some time, Missis. I heard the battle goin' on Missis, and I tought I'd stay outside the line. Haw! Haw! You know I ain't no fighter, Miss Rachel. But, Miss Rachel, dey has de trial today, don't dey?

Rachel. Yes, Tandy.

Tandy. Well, what I wanted to know is ef dey is goin' to do anything to hurt my missus cause I had to speak agin' her, can't dey take me in her place?

Rachel. I don't know, Tandy, but—

Tandy. Well, you tell 'em for me, missis; tell 'em to take me in her place and nail me up to a tree if they want to, but don't let 'em hurt missus, don't—

Rachel. (*Putting her arm around him.*) Ah, old fellow, don't be uneasy. They won't hurt Glenn or anyone else.

Tandy. Be you sure of that, Rachel?

Rachel. Very sure.

Tandy. I be powerful glad, Rachel, if dey don't. Rachel, dat is the first time anybody put their arm around old Tandy Tripp since my old mammy died. (*Exit.*)

(*Enter Reuben.*)

Reuben. Who'd ever thunk it? Well, well. Missie Glenn—she's better den all the courts and sheriffs and judges that ever tried a case. De idee! De idee ef Mars Alex's niece goin' to a court whar dey spits tobacco jooce and tells nasty tales and whar dey cyars all de weekedest fokes in de country! You mought as well take one of dem lilies and plant it in a hog pen! If dey cornvicks my little miss, old Reuben am done live long nuff! I am done lib long enuff! (*Crying.*)

(*Enter Stephen hurriedly,*)

Stephen. Uncle Reuben, where is Mr. Buck and Mr. Philip and Mr. Brockway and Dr. Zimmerman?

Reuben. Dey is all gone to de trial, Marse Stephen.

Stephen. That's so, I forgot. Uncle Reuben, when they return, be sure and tell them all not to forget to go to the polls and vote. Do you hear?

Reuben. (*Aside.*) Well, Well! And he don't keer

nuffin about Missie what loves him so hard, it just hurts my stomach to see it.

Stephen. Do you hear me, Uncle Reuben?

Reuben. Yes, sah. Mars Stephen. (*Aside*) And he's goin' workin' for his election as if it was some fer-in poor white trash as was bein' tried for stealin'·

Stephen. What's the matter with you, Uncle Reuben, that you stand there muttering to yourself?

Reuben. Marsa Stebin, Massa Stebin, it ain't for old Reuben to say nuthin' but—Massa Stebin, ain't you gwine to de court house to de trial?

Stephen. No! I haven't time. I cannot afford to be defeated in this election—I never have been defeated yet, at anything I ever attempted. My pride, my pride is at stake. I *must* win. Here, take the tickets. Give them to Mr. Philip and be sure and tell him what I've said.

Reuben. Yes, Mars Stephen. Sir—but you know Mars. Steben, what pride Mars Alex—

Stephen. Yes, yes. I know, I know. But what's that to you? (*Drums heard in the distance.*) There! There are my boys now! Don't you hear them shouting for me! Hurrah! (*Exit.*)

Reuben. And he yelled dat way like an Injun when it 'pears to me dar ought to be crape on de do'. I don't know what to make of Mars Steben since Mars Alex died now gwine on ter eight months. He never talk dat ruff to me befo'. Dey's somethin' wrong somewhar, dat's shore. Mars Alex, he always said, says he: "Thank you, Reuben," "Good mornin' Reuben," "Good night, Reuben," "Are you well, Reuben?" For forty years, too, this comin' spring he never missed it. I believe, if when he was dying, and didn't have but one breath left in his body, he'd a sed, "Thank you, thank you." (*Sighs.*) Dah! Dah dey come back from de coat house, Miss Rachel!

Rachel. Is it? Yes, they are, they are. I'm going to meet them. (*Gets her sun bonnet and runs.*)

Mary. (*At door.*) Bliss her dear heart! She's been let off! She's free! Praise all the saints!

Reuben. How does you know, Miss Mary?

Mary. Don't yer see how Rachel is a kissin' her an' goin' on and how Misther Philip is a laughing?

Reuben. Lor, dat ain't nuffin, Miss Mary, dat ain't nuffin. Mars Philip would laugh if er mule kicked him and snap his fingers as if nuthin' happened. Oh, yes, dars de doctor, laughing too, and de parson too. She's all right! Bless God! Bless God! Ef I didn't hev the rheumatiz so bad I could jest walk on my hands, I could. But, gentlemen, dat parson. Dat parson is more like human folks dan any preacher, I eber did see. I be powerful glad, Missie, I be power-ful glad Mars Philip.

(*Enter Glenn, Calvin, Doctor, Mr. Buck, Joseph and Martha.*)

Glenn. Thank you, Uncle Reuben,

Phil. Thank you, thank you. Oh, I knew there was no more danger of it Uncle Reuben than there is your refusing a piece of watermillion. Ha! Ha!

Reuben. Don't talk dat way, please Mars Philip, don't talk dat way.

Glenn. Uncle Reuben?

Reuben. Yes, marm.

Glenn. Have you seen Mr. Stephen anywhere?

Reuben. Yes'm—no'm, no'm. I haint seen him. He was bery busy and much retained down town. He—he had to help—help—help a man with a drunk-en hu-band—I mean a drunken woman—

Glenn. Uncle Reuben.

Reuben. Yes, marm.

Glenn. Look at me.

Reuben. (*Aside.*) Good Lord, I can't stand dem eyes. I can't stand dem eyes.

Glenn. Why don't you look at me, Uncle Reuben?

Reuben. Yes, marm. He said he was berry busy and—and couldn't leave and had to hurry off, and he would be in time to go to the coat house and den de tears come in his eyes, in my eyes—and he lef des tickets here for Mars Philip and Mass Buck and de parson and de doctor to be sho' and come and vote and—

Doctor. We have no right to vote yet, we have only been here eight months.

(*Exit Reuben.*)

Calvin. Yes, seven.

Buck. Philip, the polls will close at 4, we can do that much for Stephen. Let's go.

Phil. All right. Come on. (*Exit Buck and Phil.*)
(*Enter Reuben.*)

Reuben. Here's a letter whut de boy said was fer de young parson.

(*Exit Reuben.*)

Calvin. "De young parson?" All right, thank you. Hello, here's more matter for a trial.

Doctor. What is it?

Calvin. It is from my worthy board of elders. They say I must conform more strictly to the discipline of the church and that the Rev. somebody Snodgrass will be here to investigate my orthodoxy. Ha! Ha!

Rachel. The good for nothing old—

Glenn. Hush, Rachel, they think they are right.

Rachel. But, Glenn, I can't believe it. Oh, shame! I'll bet Aunt Marthy had something to do with this.

(*Aunt Martha is peeping in.*)

Calvin. By the way, Doc., they say that this Rev. Snodgrass is the one that resembles you so much.

Doctor. Is it? By George. I have some curiosity to see him.

Aunt Martha. (*Coming forward.*) But he doesn't resemble him in the least. Mr. Snodgrass has an exalted look—the appearance of a saintly man and he is the best man that ever filled a pulpit. He is an angel of goodness—

Doctor. Does he wear pants?

Aunt Martha. No. Yes, of course he does. Oh, you horrid, wicked infidel—wait 'till you see him. He'll wind you up in less than two minutes. He knows the Bible from beginning to end. You don't know anything about it. I don't believe you know anything of medicine either—no, you don't. You couldn't cure an old guinea hen!

Doctor. You haven't tried me yet. Ha! Ha! Ha!

Aunt Martha. What's he laughing about? (*Aside.*) I do believe he meant to call me a guinea hen. He think's he is awfully smart but I'll turn him down yet. (*Goes back.*)

Rachel. (*To Doctor.*) Doctor, do you want to have some fun?

Doctor. Why, yes, of course. Why?

Rachel. This old Snodgrass won't be here until tonight. Last month we had some private theatricals and Bob took part. He wore some old whiskers and a grey wig and everybody said he looked like Mr. Snodgrass, or rather old Snodgrass, for he stayed at Widow Dunlap's all last year and never paid her a cent for his board.

Doctor. Well, I'll be d—delighted. Go on.

Rachel. Now, you take that old wig and whiskers and I'll get you papa's hat and saddle-bags.

Doctor. I see—that's splendid. But how does he talk?

Rachel. (*Imitating him*) "And then you know, my dear sister, what the good book says—"

Doctor. Ha! Ha! Ha! All right.

Rachel. And then—(*Stephen says without Hurrah! Hurrah! for the invincible Stephen Venable." Enter Stephen, Philip and Buck.*)

Stephen. Hurrah! I'll be elected, my dear Martha, by the largest majority ever polled in the city.

Martha. Hurrah for the new mayor! Hurrah! Now for retrenchment, reform, etc., as usual.

Stephen. Ah, Glenn, I'm very sorry I couldn't attend your—be at the court house today, but just as I started for the fourth time, the boys would have me make a speech to the club from the 'Tenth ward" and I couldn't—

Glenn. I am very thankful that you thought of me Stephen.

Stephen. I did, I did, I assure you, and my heart ached to be with you— Ha! Yonder's some of the boys at the fence waiting to see me. Ha! Ha! Ha! I will return shortly, Glenn.

Martha, (*To Stephen.*) Stephen.

Stephen. Yes, Martha.

Martha. Hurry back at once. You are elected now. Why need you trouble any more about "the boys," as you call them?

Stephen. But they are my friends, Martha.

Martha. Well, hurry back. (*Exit Stephen.*) Friends indeed I suppose he would have such rabble as that coming into his parlor and eating at his table.

(*Enter Doctor dressed as Rev. Snodgrass.*)

Doctor. Good evening, sir, good evening. May I register my name?

Rachel. Certainly, sir. Do you wish a room?

Doctor. Yes, Missie. What do you charge for ministers of the gospel ?

Rachel. We don't sell 'em.

(*Enter Stephen.*)

Doctor. (*Snorts.*) Now, look here, Rachel, if you expect me to keep my face straight, be careful how you talk. (*Aloud.*) I mean what are your terms to the clergy ?

Rachel. Do you mean preachers ?

Doctor. Yes.

Rachel. Well, why don't you say so ? Preachers ! Well, we don't charge them any more than we charge anybody else.

Doctor. Any more ? Don't you give them the benefit of half rates ?

Rachel. Well, we might by the car load. How many have you got?

Doctor. Oh, there's only one. Can I see the proprietor of the Inn ?

Rachel. Yes, sir, you can.

Doctor. Well, where is he ?

Rachel. It ain't a he.

Doctor. Where is she, then ?

Rachel. Let me have your umbrella. Now, look right straight from that end to this end. Do you see any one?

Doctor. Yes, I see you.

Rachel. Well, you see the proprietor of this here Inn.

Doctor. What ? You ? Surely not.

Rachel. (*Slamming with her fist.*) Do you think I'd lie about it, sir?

Doctor. No, no, no, no. But you are so very young—so very young—

Rachel. How do you know I'm so very young ?

Doctor. Well, you *look* so, at least.

Rachel. How do you know I look so ? Have you seen the grey hairs in my head? Have you seen my son Benjamin that run off last week with that Larkins gal and got married ?

Doctor. I beg your pardon, Missy—or Mrs. B—B—B—B—Buck.

Rachel. Don't call me, Mrs. Buck.

Doctor. Will you forgive me if I respectfully and submissively inquire how I shall address you?

Rachel. Yes. Call me Colonel.

Doctor. (*Smiling.*) Colonel?

Rachel. Yes, and be quick about it; I'm busy.

Doctor. Will you please assign me what room you please, Colonel?

Rachel. Yes. 2040.

Doctor. 2040!

Rachel. Yes, we begin up and come down.

Doctor. May I go *up*?

Rachel. (*In old primer style.*) May you go up? You may go up. You may also go down.

Doctor. (*To Stephen.*) What a remarkable person! (*Aloud.*) I beg your pardon, but does one Mr. Brockway live far from here?

Rachel. Not very easily.

Doctor. You do not seem to catch my meaning. Does Mr. Brockway live very far from the Inn.

Rachel. He can't.

Doctor. Why?

Rachel. Because he lives right there on that chair.

Doctor. Ah! This is Mr. Brockway, is it?

Calvin. Yes, sir. (*Aside.*) He does resemble old Doc. sure enough. (*Aloud.*) And you are—

Doctor. The Rev. Ipecac Snodgrass, sir.

Calvin. Ah, indeed. Mr. Snodgrass, I'm—(*extending his hand which the Rev. S. refuses to take.*)

Doctor. I cannot take your hand yet sir, until I discover whether or not the charges preferred against you be true.

Calvin. Very well, sir. I have no objection to that I have been apprised by my board of—elders that an investigation would be held and that you would appear to decide the matter temporarily.

Doctor. Temporarily, sir? I can assure you, sir, that whatever my action may be, sir, it will be approved by the Synod, sir.

Calvin. Ah? May I ask what charges have been preferred against me, sir?

Doctor. The charges will be submitted in detail at the meeting tomorrow morning at 7 o'clock.

Calvin. At seven?

Doctor. Yes, sir, at seven. I see you are surprised at such an early hour. That is conclusive that you do not ordinarily rise 'till later,—say 8 or half past 8 in the morning ?

Calvin. You are correct, sir.

Doctor. And therefore you do not retire 'till midnight or after ?

Calvin. Yes, sir.

Doctor. I begin to fear the charges are true.

Calvin. Would you object to stating those charges now ?

Doctor. Yes, sir. The examination, according to Sec. 4, Art. 32, of the discipline of the church, must be held behind locked doors. At least that's the way I understand it, and the moderator says I am correct. Says he, "Snodgrass, you are right, you are always right !"

Calvin. These are all my friends here, sir. I haven't the slightest fear from them or anyone else on earth for that matter.

Doctor. The charges are of a very serious nature, sir—(*Aunt Marthy is peeping in.*)—and

Calvin. Serious ? What do you mean by serious ? Charges of immorality ? .

Doctor. Yes, sir.

Calvin. Say what the charges are.

Doctor. I cannot do so according to the discipline 'till tomorrow, sir.

Calvin. (*Rising and taking off his coat.*) I'll just give you three seconds to begin. (*Rachel laughs.*)

Doctor. (*Aside.*) By George ! I'll find a black eye religiously put on if I don't take care, (*Aloud*) Well, sir, the first is that you rise late in the morning and sit up or are up late at night.

Calvin. Well, sir, what of that ? Have I committed burglary or petit larceny ?

Doctor. O, no, no, no. That is, not that I am aware of sir. But I hold, sir that it is conduct unbecoming a minister to go about at midnight—

Calvin. About what?

Doctor. About anything, sir. Why, sir, we are credibly informed that in Paris, the most ungodly city on earth, people seldom go to bed before midnight.

Calvin. Well, sir, what of that ?

Doctor. What of it, sir? Don't you know it is French and therefore immoral, sir?

Calvin. "French and therefore immoral," is it? (*Aside*) well, I do wonder if he is such a hopeless fool as that. (*Aloud*). Go on.

Doctor. I understand also that you prefer your dinners in courses, sir after the manners of those of this modern Sodom and Gomorrah?

Calvin. I prefer my dinner in courses? Yes.

Doctor And that, too, sir is French and therefore immoral.

Calvin. And these are some of your serious charges, are they?

Doctor. I have not done yet, sir.

Calvin. Well, go on. (*Aside*). He begins to amuse me.

Doctor. You are charged with driving a fast horse too, sir.

Calvin. Yes, sir. He is of the best blood of all the stables of Kentucky. But he has never been trained for the race track. I don't know what his speed is. He is very sensible, sir; knows my voice and loves me, too.

Doctor. That's it sir. The church holds it immoral and worldly to own a race-horse and very unbecoming to drive faster than an easy trot.

Calvin. Well, how may I hope to ever be forgiven? But, go on.

Doctor. You are accused of bringing into church a number of children whom nobody knows, and whose fathers and mothers nobody knows, thereby bringing them in contact with the children of respectable and well-known people.

Calvin. Can you find a child, sir, that God would disown?

Doctor. He disowns all those that are not converted.

Calvin. (*Strongly.*) I differ from you, sir.

Doctor. And the Church differs from you, sir,

Calvin. I don't believe it, sir.

Doctor. And that is not all, sir. You are accused of going into whiskey shops and saloons, sir, to bring them out, sir.

Calvin. Yes, sir, it is true.

Doctor. And you have been seen looking on at a dance! Aha! Aha!

Calvin. I made no effort to hide! Aha! Aha!

Doctor. Do you mock me, sir? That also is very unbecoming.

Calvin. And you, sir, are unbecoming to everything, everywhere. Do you understand that, sir?

Doctor. Be calm, sir, be calm. This quick and irascible temper is very characteristic of the French, I learn.

Calvin. The poor French! Yes, it is.

Doctor. There's the danger, sir, there's the danger. You are charged also with laughing at some woman's clothes which you saw on a clothes-line, sir?

Calvin. Ha! Ha! Yes, sir, I did. Should I have taken off my hat to them?

Doctor. You should have looked away, sir.

Calvin. Bah! (*Aside*) who could have known anything of that but Doc Zimmerman? By the way, Miss Glenn— Oh, Rachel, where is Dr. Zimmerman?

Doctor. (Whispering), Hush. Not a word:

(*Calvin recognizes him, is much surprised, motions as if to strike him in fun, when Aunt Martha, comes forward.*)

Calvin. Have you done sir?

Doctor. Yes, sir. For the present. But I'd advise you to go to bed early tonight. Why, who's this?

Aunt Martha. Why, Brother Snodgrass, don't you know—

Doctor. Sister Marthy! Well, well! well! I be very glad to see you, sister Marthy.

Aunt Martha. How much younger you do look, Brother Snodgrass! The blue grass region seems to agree with you.

Doctor. Well, yes You see, sister Marthy, since Maria died and left me I have been mighty lonely—

Aunt Marthy. Your wife? Is she dead? O, now, what a pity! What a pity!

Doctor. Yes, sister Marthy, she was a mighty good woman, er-Maria was a mighty good woman, sister Marthy.

Aunt Marthy. What was her disease, poor Brother Snodgrass?

Doctor. She had—what the devil did she have?

(*Enter Mary Gary with Glenn. Glenn is laughing merrily.*)

Mary. Why, Miss Glenn, they be the out-doinest little devils I iver saw.

Stephen. What's the matter now, Mary?

Mary. Them little twins ye brought here, Masther Stephen.

Stephen. What have they done?

Mary. Why I went in last noight to give them a bath. I took one of them into the bath room and washed him and then put a gown on him and put him to bed. Then I had to go to the kitchen a little toime and thin I come back for the other one, when I took him by the hand, they both begun to laugh. "What ye laughin at?" says I. But they kept on laughing. I took him in and washed him in could water and sure it was enough to make him sarious but he kept on laughing What ye laughing at?" says I, but he ke kept on laughing, and when I took him back ter the room they both laughed and laughed like they would break their little ribs. Then—what do you think? They tould me I had washed one of them twice and hadn't washed the other one at all, at all. (*Exit Mary.*) (*All 'augh, Dor or laughs so hearily that ne is discovered by Aunt Martha.*)

Aunt Martha. Oh, you horrid thing!

Doctor. Ha! Ha! Ha! Why where's brother Snodgrass? Has anybody seen brother Snodgrass?

Calvin. Rachel, where is brother Snodgrass?

Rachel. Philip, where is brother Snodgrass?

Phil. (*Looking out of door*) Where's brother Snodgrass? (*Exit Aunt Martha.*)

Rachel. Here's the mail. Give it to me, Uncle Reuben. (*Enter Uncle Reuben.*)

Martha. Anything for me, Rachel?

Rachel. (*Calling them off*) Philip Breen, Rev. Calvin—Rev. Calvin—Dr. Zimmerman, Philip—Rev. Calvin—Miss Martha Delmar—(*gives it to her*) from New York, too, in a large envelope!

Now what does that mean? Buck, Buck, Simpson, Torrey, Miss Glenn—Here's one for you, Glenn.

Pshaw! where's mine? This looks like it. Pshaw! Mrs. Martha—and there's another—Miss Mary Gary —Robert Buck, Jr. That's from his girl up at Mill's Landing that straightened his cravat for him in church the second time she ever met him—such Yankee impudence! Miss Lillie Rose White. Miss who? Oh, yes, that's our cook. She's as black as the ace of spades. And many papers which I will, with my superior educational accomplishments, proceed to assort.

Glenn. Come, Calvin, let us walk on the veranda— (*Exit Calvin and Glenn.*)

Martha. Stephen?

Stephen. Yes.

Martha. Come here. Pick up my gloves. I have a letter here from New York.

Stephen. Be careful. Rachel is listening.

Martha. I see. And Philip only pretends to be involved in deep study as he walks the   to and fro. I talk for their benefit and yours, too. (*Aloud.*) Ha! Ha! Ha! The foolish fellow. I met him at school and on his return to New York where his father is a Banker—(*whispering*) I must receive no more letters from that Bank—Rachel observed it suspiciously—(*Aloud as Phillip and Rachel pass*)—Ha! Ha! Why he actually made love to me the first time I met him!

Stephen. I wish they would stop that incessant walking.

Martha Think of it, Stephen, (*whispering*). You must do all this correspondence yourself. They will not suspect you. (*Aloud*). He said he had loved me always. Ha! Ha! Had seen me in his dreams! Ha! Ha! Ha!

Stephen Ha! Ha! Ha!

Martha Don't laugh so loud—they will come in to share the fun.

Stephen. I'd rather not laugh at all, God knows.

Martha. Bah! There's your tender conscience again. (*Aloud.*) And he's a poet too. Just look at this! Ha! Ha! (*Whispering.*) They send letters of credit and have forwarded check book, &c.

Stephen. How are you to check on this deposit?

Martha. (*Aloud.*) Why, yes I promised him everything—he was such a calf! Said he must have known me in another life! Ha! Ha! Ha!

Stephen. Asked you if you believed in the doctrine of reminiscence, eh! Ha! Ha! (*Aside.*) This laughing tears my very soul at every breath.

Martha. Why, yes. Ha! Ha! (*Whispering.*) It must not be done. Let it remain there.

Stephen. Did you cut out that leaf from the Register?

Martha. Yes, and I h   since learned that Chas. K. Withers, Jr., whose name we used, is dead.

Stephen. Ah! (*Deep sigh.*)

Martha. (*Aside.*) That's a lie. But it is a kind one, also. I do it for the sake of his conscience which is as tender as a new born babe.

Stephen. What did you do with the leaf!

Martha. (*Aloud.*) Ha! Ha! Ha! Do you suppose I keep all such nonsense? Ha! Ha!

Stephen. Why, no, you are right.

Martha. (*Whispering.*) And Withers lived at Trenton, New Jersey. If they should trace the correspondence to him— (*Aloud.*) And he says he will send me a diamond ring if I will accept it—Ha! Ha! If I will accept it! He's a real mush-poultice. Ha!

Phil. (*At door.*) How happy they are! Ah! If my Susanna were only—(*Walks on*).

Martha. (*Aside.*) At Mesopotamia, for all I care.

Stephen. And do you really mean to accept his ring?

Martha. What? A diamond ring? Why not? This is one of the reminiscences, you know. Besides, I will write him afterwards that I care nothing for the ring except as a token of his deep love for me and regret very much to return it. Then, out of sentiment he will write that—

Stephen. (*Looking around*). I smell something burning somewhere, don't you?

Martha. Some old rags in the back yard, I suppose.

Stephen. And when, dear Martha, when will you be my wife?

Martha. Oh, that day will come, you may be sure.

Stephen. But when, my girl, oh, when?

Martha. Oh, there's no hurry. Besides, I do not

know that you will keep your oath— You seem to
grow weaker in your nerves instead of stronger. Just
look at me.   For your dear sake and the possibilities
you are capable of I could look at all the eyes of the
earth, and yes, such as might arise from their graves
and with the frightened innocence of child-hood say:
"I don't know, sir."   "I never heard of it—"

Stephen.   What's that noise?

Martha.   It's that Mary Gary's voice,   Quarreling
with Aunt Marthy, I'll warrant.

Stephen.   No, it isn't.   It's fire!

Mary.   (*Without.*)   Hurry up, Uncle Reuben. Bring
some water quick.

Phil.   (*Without.*)   What is it Mary?

Mary.   (*Without*)   It's fire, Misther Philip, and in
your room, too.

Phil.   What! all my costly furniture?   (*runs up
stairs.*)

Martha.   Now, see how excited you are.

Stephen.   Do you want the house to burn down?
(*Exit hurriedly.*)

(*Glenn and Rachel hurry past the door carrying buckets of water—Cal and Doc run past with coats off*).

Calvin.   (*Without.*)   Smother it out, Phil.   Smother it out!

Mary.   (*Without.*)   Lookout down below there!   (*She
throws out Philip's bric-a brac, boot-jack, old hats,
chairs and table.*)

Calv n.   (*Without.*)   It's all out, all out.   (*Enter
Phil—hurriedly.*)   (He is coatless and his shirt sleeves
are torn.   Enter Mary also with two empty water-
buckets in one hand, a broom in the other.   Her face
is black with smut.   Her sleeves are rolled high and
her arms are black.)

Phil.   Where's my trunk?   Where is my manuscript and trousseau?

Mary.   It's done burnt up, Misther Phillip, bad
luck to it.

Phil.   Don't say so, Mary, don't say so.

Mary.   Don't say so, is it?   It's nobody I'd tell a
lie for sooner than for you, Mr. Philip, but it's done
burnt up, Mr. Philip.

Phil.   Well, well, well!   (*Sinking into chair.*)   The
accumulated fortunes of years of hard work!   All

gone in a measly little five minutes? (*Pause.*) Humph! (*snapping his fingers*). Well, if that don't beat the devil!

Martha. Pshaw! He suffers like a hog and with no more feeling.

Phil. Well, I'm not dead yet. And my Susan's wedding garments, too. And all my little pets broken, scattered. Now, there's saint Peter I carved so patiently— His nose is gone and St. Paul with one ear off—and James with both arms gone, and there's Judas. How are you, Judas? He was the one I loved most because everybody else despised him. Ah! He is safe! Not a scratch! Not a scratch! (*Looking reflectively at them all.*) Now, my saintly gentlemen, any one would think you had been in the devil of a scrimmage up-stairs! Ha! Ha! Why, where's good old bland, bald-headed St. Vincent de Paul with two little foundling babes, one in each arm. I carved him when I had the mumps and couldn't go out. Ah! Here's half of him. Split square half and half from top to bottom. With only one eye, half a nose, half a head, one arm and one leg, he still holds on to the baby. There's pluck for you! hurrah! for St. Vincent de Paul. Ha! Ha?

Mary. And it was mesilf, Mr. Phillip as come along the hall and smelling smoke I looked into No. 14 and didn't see it and then I looked into No. 15 and didn't see it and then I looked into No. 16, and didn't see it, and then I looked into No. 17 and didn't see it, and then I looked into No. 18 and didn't see it &c.

Phil. And you found it in No. 26.

Mary: (*Not hearing.*) And I looked into No. 20 and didn't see it, but surely I thought it must be in No. 21.

Phil. Where was it burning, Mary, did the trunk catch first?

Mary. No. It wasn't in No. 22; and I kipt on lookin' and lookin' and says I, "I'd rather not find it in Mr. Philip's room because the saints watch over him—he is so blessed good."

Phil. Mary! Mary! That's enough.

Mary. And it was himself that helped me mother carry the pig over the crake down by—

Phil. (*Taking her by the arm.*) **The cook** is calling you·

Mary. All right, all right, Misther Philip. May the blissid saints give you a new trunk and a whole pile of writin' and another suit of weddin' clothes. (*Exit Mary.*)

(*Philip is busy "repairing his fortunes."*)

Rachel. · Why, here's a letter without any address at all. And in one of our envelopes. Now, what blazed-faced, wall-eyed idiot could have done that? But how am I going to find out? Why, I'll have to open it, of course. Lookout secrets. Hide your heads, for Rachel's after you. (*Opens it.*) "Dear Mr. Withers. Why, that's my own letter and I didn't address it. Dog—dog—Oh I wish I was a man, a regular tough, so I could cuss it in good style. Hold on! Hold on! No; I don't. Why this is the one I didn't want to send. And he didn't get it after all. Ah. Thank you, thank you. You are so sweet. (*Kissing the blank envelope.*) And here's a letter from him, the very last in the pile. (*Tearing it open with a rim.*) I'll teach you to keep me waiting this way again— "My Little Darling"—(*Long sigh.*) (*She then reads the letter in pantomime with many smiles, quiet laughter. gestures, etc.*) What? "Will leave for the blessed Sunny South tomorrow." Then he'll be here tomorrow! Oh, I'm so happy! I could just kiss—(*Kisses her hand, her arm, her apron, the letter, the register, the desk the wall*)—everybody. (*Enter Aunt Martha.*) Oh, Aunt Marthy, I love you! (*Kisses her.*)

Aunt Martha. Child, child. Are you crazy? Don't you know that kissing is a very foolish practice?

Rachel. Yes, Aunt Marthy, I'm crazy. I'm hopelessly insane! (*Laughs.*)

Aunt Martha. Rachel, where is the Christian Observer?

Rachel. He's well.

Aunt Martha. I ask, where is the Christian Observer.

Rachel. Oh, I wrapped up some spoiled mackerel with it.

Aunt Martha. Oh, you impious wretch! Spoiled mackerel in a Christian Observer. Bah!

Rachel. Aunt Marthy, do you think it will make him sick?

Aunt Martha. Make who sick?

Rachel. The Observer. Ha! Ha!

Aunt Martha. Bah!

Rachel. Better to make him sick than the boarders. Oh, my Charlie, my Charlie, fly, fly. fly to me. I don't just believe I can stand it. I don't believe—
(*Enter Uncle Reuben peeping in at the door.*)

Reuben. Honey. Honey. Ahem! He's down at de gate and wants to see yer.

Rachel. Who?

Reuben. Dat white Yankee!

Rachel. Look out! (*Jumps over desk and rushes through door.*

Reuben. Hyah! Hyah! Hyah! I ain't felt so good since I had my head shampooled—Hyah! Hyah! (*Exit.*)

(*Enter Glenn, meeting Stephen.*)

Glenn. Well, somebody's happy, anyway.

Stephen. Who!

Glenn. Rachel.

Stephen. Why?

Glenn. Her sweetheart's come.

Stephen. Who is he?

Glenn His name is Charlie Withers.

Stephen. Withers? Where from?

Glenn. Trenton, New Jersey, I think. Why. what's the matter? Do you know anything against him?

Stephen. No, no, no. I thought—I was thinking of another matter just then.

Glenn. Oh, I'm so glad, so glad. (*Exit.*)

(*Enter Rachel.*)

Rachel. Yes, I'll register for him. If I can write the sweetest name on earth—"Chas. J. Withers, Jr., and wife"—Oh, Ha! Ha! what am I doing? He must drive to the farm and see Bob tonight. Ah, there's his buggy—I must have one more. (*Making noise of many kisses with her mouth.*) (*Exit.*)

(*Enter Martha.*)

Stephen. Martha!

Martha. Yes?

Stephen. Look at the register.

Martha. (*Imitating him.*) Look at the register! Are there any ghosts there?

Stephen. Yes

Martha. (*Tiptoeing with long stealthy strides.*) Who fears? I'm a ghost myself. Ha! Ha! "Chas. J. Withers, Jr." Indeed! And you stand there as if your bones were made of sausage-meat.

Stephen. What should I do?

Martha, Go call him aside, tell him there's a warrant for his arrest in the hands of the sheriff. That he must fly and never come back.

Stephen. But there's no warrant.

Martha. Go. Go. If you love me Stephen. (*Exit Stephen.*) No sooner did I see that postmark "Trenton, N. J." than I began to watch. I learned from Rachel that he was coming. I found a boy to take a message to the sheriff, using Mr. Buck's signature—(*looking through door.*) Ah! Stephen has told him. He seems to expostulate, Stephen begs him—he gets in—he drives rapidly—that's the "Early Bird" he's driving, a good horse—(*Enter Stephen.*)

Stephen. I am glad there is no warrant for him in the hands of that rash and hot-headed sheriff. He would shoot him with the slightest resistance. (*Rachel enters at door and dances and hugs an imaginary lover, etc.*)

Martha. (*Aside.*) That's just what I want. (*To Stephen.*) Now, look how nervous you are.

Stephen. I can't help it, Martha. I feel very strangely over this affair of Wither's. I must go after him. (*Rushing out.*)

Martha. Stephen!

Stephen. Yes.

Martha. Come here. Remember your invariable luck. With it you can have everything you wish for. (*Aside.*) How dangerously happy Rachel is! I was mistaken in her! She will suffer beautifully! Now, now you look better, Stephen. You can smile again.

Stephen. Yes, yes, so I can.

(*Enter messenger boy with note for Stephen.*)

Boy. Here's a note for you, "Steben."

Stephen. Ha! That's Larry; one of my partners. How are you Larry?

Boy. Oh, I'm bully. Are you bully?

Stephen. Ha! Ha! Yes, I'm bully, too.

Calvin. Why, Larry, what tore your pants so?

Larry. Dat old nigger's dog got after me and run me uper tree—dad gash him!

(*Exit Larry.*)

Stephen. Hurrah! The count stands 1,114 major-ity, Martha, for Venable! 1,114! Hurrah! From the Mayoralty to the Legislature is an easy step—then higher to the Governor's chair! Beyond that to Congress! Beyond that to the Senate Chamber! And still higher to the noblest of all earthly dignities! My darling Martha! Ha! Ha! Ha! What is it we cannot win? With health and strength and friends and my lucky star ever kindly beaming over me and my Queen's genius to help me—Ha! Ha! Ha! (*A voice from the air.*) And the Midland Bonds, too.

Stephen. (*Startled.*) Yes, yes. I forgot. I—

Martha. (*Aside*). Now comes one of his spells again.

Stephen. (*Stephen is violently shaken.*) Will that walking never cease?

Martha. Let me observe the twitching of that muscle. Delightful! Delightful! What a glorious subject he is! A quivering mass of shattered nerves. I have discovered a freak in human anatomy. No bones, no blood, no cartilage, nothing but nerves, and I can play upon them all.

Stephen. You love me, don't you, Martha?

Martha. Of course I do, Stephen.

Stephen. Then let everything sound that can make a noise. Let forth the sad voice of eternal woe, I will be merry. I will laugh in spite of everything on the earth, or under it, or over it, or outside of it—my Martha loves me! Ha! Ha! Ha! Ah! (*Long, painful sigh. Pause, during which he suffers agony.*) Doctor.

Doctor. (*Coming to him.*) What is it, Stephen?

Stephen. (*Slowly.*) Can't you cut out my ears?

Doctor. (*To Calvin.*) I don't like those symptoms. He must have a change.

CURTAIN.

ACT 3d.

SCENE.—*Interior of Ship "Seagull." Large door at Back center, showing rail without and the Sea. Time, night. Table at L. C. Sofa Lounge on L. Chairs, etc. Table on R. where four gamblers are seated playing cards and drinking, Stephen is discovered watching game as curtain rises. Glenn is busy, bustling about.*

Stephen. What on earth are you driving at, Glenn?

Glenn. I'm preparing for the ball.

Stephen. What ball?

Glenn. Mrs. Murkin's ball.

Stephen. And who is Mrs. Murkins?

Glenn. Mrs. Murkins is Polly. You see I thought it would be something novel to the little tots that never knew anything but squalor and rough usages to let them play little men and women for once in their lives. Some of them have been sea-sick too and the trip to Australia is so long—

Stephen. Delightful idea! Glenn, you are an angel. But look.—(*Enter Mollie, Davie and Pansy, the girls carrying dresses in their hands and Davie, in stocking feet—one sock on, other off, and holding coat in his hand. As they enter, they cry, saying:* "Yes, and I'm going to tell Miss Glenn, too, Yes, I am! Miss Glenn, what do you think? That nasty Larry went and tied up all our close!

Glenn. Hush! Hush! We can fix all that. You musn't come out here. This is Miss Murkins' ball room, and she is almost ready. She must'nt find you here. Go on, now, and I'll straighten your clothes for you. (*Exeunt children.*) I'll see how the Murkinses are getting on Ah, here they come. (*Enter Taddy as Mrs. Murkins and Polly as Miss Indiana Murkins*) Good evening Mrs. Murkins, Miss Polly, I

must congratulate you upon the propitious circum-
stances attendant upon your brilliant debut into
Washington society.

Mrs. Murkins. (*Fanning herself with slow dignity.*)
With pleasure. No, dat aint it.

Glenn. Say I thank you.

Miss M. I tank you.

Glenn. Bow slightly and smile sweetly.

Mrs. M. Bow slightly and smile sweetly. Can't
you smile? Not that way. Now, watch me.

Glenn. Now, Mrs. Murkins, you and Miss Murkins must stand just here and you most hold your
heads high like real Aristocrats. And don't forget
to say "loff" and "holf-post" for no one can tell what
State you came from unless you do.

Mrs. M. When muster say dat?

Glenn. Whenever it occurs in your conversation.

Mrs. M. (*To Miss M.*) Dat means when youse
talkin', Polly.

Glenn. Don't call her Polly. Say. My daughter.

Miss M. I wonder why Fidget don't come?

Glenn. No, that aint the way I taught you to say
it.

Miss M. Oh, I ferdot. (*Walking about.*) O, dear,
O, dear, what can detain that girl? I am as nervous
as I tan be. She promised to be here and help me
receive my guests. Oh, my Dear Mother. What
shall I do? I—I.

Glenn. Do believe—

Miss M. Do believe—Oh, yeth? Do believe my
guests are coming, and that odious creature has not
arrived yet— Ah, there she is? You darling sweet
girl, (*kissing her rapidly*) you have come just in time.
How do I look?

Fidget. Just too sweet for anything. I declare
that lace is lovely. And how do I look?

Miss M. Gaugeous! Dazzlin'. Atroshus!

Glenn. Oh, No, No, No. That doesn't come in
there.

Stephen Ha! Ha! Ha! God bless her little tongue

Glenn. Here they come, Miss Fidget. No, I was
mistaken.

(*Stephen is standing by gambling table*)

Stephen. Ha! Ha! I can direct Goozle's hand

which is rather unsteady as you see, gentlemen, and beat the whole crowd.

1st Gambler. You direct nuthin' but yourself, Pard.

2nd Gam. Have yer got any dust in yer close?

Stephen. Yes, and I won't touch the cards, either.

1st Gam. All right. Come on. Dar'll be lambs wool scattered round so you can lay down on it and sleep. (*They shuffle and deal.*)

Stephen. (*Aside.*) He's young in years, but if it were possible to fleece him, Tandy Tripp couldn't sleep on the wool.

Goozle. You sthand in wid dem?

Stephen. I'll pay for what you lose. And if you lose anything, I agree to walk home—Ha! Ha! That's a good hand. No not that. Now. This one. See? Ours. Again. Play. Yes, that's good.

1st Gam. Raise de limit?

Stephen. Yes.

1st Gam. How much?

Stephen. Five.

1st Gam. Ten.

Stephen. Twenty.

2nd Gam. Forty.

Stephen. Fifty.

1st Gam. Call.

Stephen. Show up. Ah! ours.

Goozle. Ha! Ha! You take half (hic) pard, and I take balaush.

Stephen. No, No. I don't want— (*Enter Aunt Martha.*

Aunt Martha. Oh, horrors! Stephen, Stephen, what do you mean?

Stephen. I am not gambling, Aunt Martha.

Aunt M. Come away from the horrible wretches. I was afraid there would be just such a scene as this if I didn't come.

1st Gam. (*Aside.*) The governor don't know me. Then I'm safe at school. Ha! Ha? Ha!

Stephen. But Aunt—

Aunt M. Come Stephen you must not.

Goozle. Come, Steben, old fel—

Aunt M. The beasts! Come my boy.

Stephen. (*Sighing.*) Oh, Aunt Martha, you that

condemn the gambler, little can you know what pow-
ers of hellish magic work upon him.

Goozle. (*Who has got between Stephen and Aunt
M—*) Shtephen, have a drink? I shay, have a drink?
(*placing it to Aunt M's nose. She hasn't observed him
following.*)

Aunt M. Bah! (*Exit, pulling out Stephen who laughs
heartily.*)

Goozle. (*Realizing his error.*) Ha! Ha! Ha! (*Returning.*) Damnish fellow, too.

Glenn Here they come, here they come, Introduce them, Fidget.

Fidget. Aw, Mitter Kildee and Miss Van Sope!
Delighted to see you. Judge Squander and Miss
McTubb. Capt. Snob and Miss Hamgravy. Squire
Hawks and Miss Puddin'—

Glenn. Gingerbread!

Fidget. Ha! Ha! Dats so. I ferdot. I knowd it
was something dood. Sir Gerald Fopp and Miss
Swipeall.— Hon. Always Dry and Miss Rickety.
Ladies and gentlemen, permit me to interjooce to you
our gracious hostess and her charmin' daughter—
Mrs. Murkins and Miss Murkins. (*All bow very low*)
was dat right?

Glenn. Ha! Ha! Ha! Dat was right. (*Enter at
door, Calvin. Dr. Z—Philip and Stephen*).

Calvin. Hello! What's all this?

Stephen. Some of Glenn's work you may rely on it.
(*All the men laugh.*).

Glenn. Judge Squander?

Judge S. (*Swelling pompously*). Mrs. Murkins, allow
me to congratulate you—look here missie, I don't want
no more mug twisters like dat.

Glenn. Go on.

Judge S. Upon being the mammy or mother of
much transcendent loveliness as we see before us.
Whew!

Mrs. M. Tank you Judge Squander. De wisdom
of de bench does honor to our fragile muliebrity.

Judge S. Gee whiz! What did she say?

Glenn. Ha! Ha! That's right. Now, Capt.
Snob.

Capt. S. Madam, I am constrained to say that this

thrilling occasion reminds me of my visit to England about four years ago, when—

All. Ahem! ahem! Oh, Oh, Oh. (*Judge S. places his hands on his stomach as if in colic.*)

Capt. S. I was interjooced ter one of deir old generals whose name was Billington, or Wellington and everybody called him Juke. He grasped my hand very warmly and said he was delighted to meet the gallant young American Captain of whose daring valor he had heard so much. I told him I *thought* I had heard of him too. (*Strutting away and twirling his mustache.*)

Mrs. M. Ha! Ha! You served him right, Captain.

Squire H. I don't engenerally invite no city folks to my house widout consultin' er Mandy, for Mandy would jest bile ef she knowd I was skippin an gallivauntin round such temtations as Miss Gingerbread here, but ef ye ever come down my way, I'll meet ye at de landin' wid my four horse wagin.

Mrs. M. Squire Hawks, I should be delighted to avail myself.

Hon, A. D. My Dear Madam, I been ten years in Congress and have saw America's beauty and chivalry pass before my eyes like a panorama. I must say I have never saw more consounded grace—

Glenn. Consummate grace.

Hon. A. D. Con— What?

Glenn. Consummate.

Hon. A. D. Consummate grease— Grease, Ha! Ha!

All. Grease! Ha! Ha! Ha!

Hon. A. D. (*To Judge.*) What is you laffin' fer, Kid? You never done no better. (*Judge continues to laugh, when Hon. A. D. kicks him.*)

Glenn. Now, now, Mr. Dry. I'm ashamed of you.

Squire H. He aint no count, no way, cordin' to my tell. Dars de State Bank law.—

Hon. A. D. My dear sir, you forget I have done appointed four men in your county to office—

Squire. But dad blast it, sir, dem little offices don't do do *people* no good. De State Bank law—

Hon. A. D. The State Bank Law be squashed—

Squire. But, sir, de constitution—

Hon. A. D. De constitution be ramfoozled, sir. I'll be elected again, sir, in spite of your opposition, sir. What difference does it make, sir, if the whole country is ruined, sir? Aint I done been re-elected and aint I done got all the offices for you I could? My Godelmighty! Some folks wouldn't be satisfied wid gold wash-tubs.

Fidget. Be talm, Dentermens, be talm. Permit de sergin' billows of your legislative brains to sleep. De rule is de fust one dat gits mad shant have no ice-cream.— now!

Hon. A. D. What?

Fidget. I meant no champain. (*Hon. A. D. & Squire H. embrace.*)

Miss Rickety. Aw, is we doin to have some ice tream?

All. Miss Glenn, are we doing to have some sho' nuff?

Glenn. Yes, yes, but you must dance first.

Fidget. Be pleased ladies and gentlemen to prepare for the dance.

(*They arrange themselves in couples and dance the minuet.*)

Fidget. Oh, Miss Glenn, let Billy Kildee dance.

Glenn. Billy? Why, he has been dancing.

Fidget. I mean Billy's dance. Please, Missie.

Glenn. All right. Go ahead Billy.

Billy. Which one!

Fidget. Dat one what Uncle Ben learned you out on de plantation.

Billy. De cotton field dance? All right. (*Music starts, Billy begins but stops suddenly.*) I beg your pardon. I dance with your sweet permission?

Mrs. M. Certainly, Mr. Kildee. (*Billy dances.*) (*They all pat for him.*)

Glenn. Come, now, Fidget, invite them to the supper room.

Fidget. Gentlemen. be kind enough to escort the ladies to the supper room. (*They go out hurriedly and promiscously. yelling and whooping.*) (*Glenn follows*)

Stephen. God bless their little hands, heads, fingers and toes!

Doctor. Amen!

Aunt M. Yes, I'm not surprised to hear you say amen to anything that is worldly and sinful.

Calvin. Why, Aunt Martha, you surely do not see any harm in that?

Aunt M. And you don't appear to see harm in anything. When they are grown, they'll think of nothing but dancing and waltzing and flirting and dallying on the very verge of eternal perdition. But you don't believe in that, either.

Calvin. No Aunt Martha, I do not.

Aunt M. Dont you believe the Bible at all?

Calvin. I prefer not to discuss it, Aunt Martha.

Aunt M. The Bible says, "he that believeth not shall be damned."

Calvin. The Bible seems to teach what you believe. But it cannot mean that, Aunt Martha. If it did it would be not only not divine in some of its parts but positively inhuman and fiendish as the devil himself.

Aunt M. Oh, you wicked, profane creature. I'm glad you will be excommunicated. I'll not stay to listen to such blasphemy. (*Exit.*)

Calvin. Now, I'm sorry I said that. For, like many others, she will misunderstand me. That's the danger. In discarding certain statements in the Bible as of human error and not of divine origin, they are apt to throw it all away, reckless of the priceless gems that sparkle there.

Stephen. You intend resigning the ministry, Calvin?

Calvin. Yes.

Stephen. You will not meet your trial then?

Calvin. Oh! yes.

Stephen. Why

Calvin. To defy every -eye that gazes upon the clear record of my deeds.

Stephen. You are right.

Calvin. I shall part with the old church in sorrow. But I can no longer preach such doctrine as they believe, and I will not. They think they are right, and I think that I am right. Of some things, however, I am sure. The husbandry of Heaven spares the tree that stands laden with fruit. If half the fruit be rotten, it is spared for the other half. If all be rotten but one single apple, divine mercy spares it for that. If all be rotten and the tree itself decayed, divine wisdom sees the barren soil in which it grew, the storms that blasted it, the frosts that withered it, the worms that consumed it, and Divine Pity, yes, and divine justice too spares even the rotten tree!

Philip. How magnificent is the ocean. And what creatures of microscopic life are men when borne upon its mighty waves!

Doctor. Right genteel thing, the ocean is.

Stephen. Right genteel! You have a better one in England, I suppose?

Doctor. Ha! Ha! Ha! I hope not.

Phil. But you do love it, don't you Doc? Say you love something for the Lord's sake.

Doctor. Of course I do. That is, I do *now*. I didn't last night, about midnight. It is the grandest thing beneath the stars. It is—

Goozle. Whutshat? The ocean? Oh, ish beautiful! Ish perfecly buful! (Hic) I aint got but one (hic) objections to it. And (hic) the worst of it is there don't seem to be any way to (hic) remedy it.

Doctor. What's that?

Goozle. Why (hic) don't shee? The hull dam shing is made er *water*! (hic) (his "gorge rises" at the thought.)

All. Ha! Ha! Ha!

Phil. (*At door.*) Ah, here come our little friends.

Calvin. And they all have on their gowns. They must not come in here.

Stephen. Yes, yes, why not? They are nothing but children.

Phil. They stand timidly waiting for an invitation.

Stephen. Come in, come right in, ladies. (*Enter children.*) Ah, good evening, Miss Van Sope. Miss Rickety, I believe? (*bowing very low.*) You were never arrayed half so beautifully. Miss Fidget, may I claim the next dance with you? Oh, thank you.

Doctor. (*Who has been stretched on sofa.*) Ha! Ha! Ha! Just look at 'em. Hello Fidget, come here. Roost on my shoulder. (*He places Fidget on his shoulder, and then Fidget, flapping her arms, crows like a chicken. All laugh. Doctor laughs and kisses her. Then he lies on the floor on his back.*)

Fidget. Pile on! pile on! (*All the children pile on him, laughing and screaming.*) (*Then Fidget wants to jump over him*). Oh, Docter. You is dest right to dump over.

Stephen. Come, now, tots. Your little song. Come, Fidget, we are going to sing now. Fidget!

Fidget. Oh, please, Teven, lemme have one more dump.

Stephen. All right. (*She spits on her hands,, takes a "running start" and tries to jump over Doctor's stomach, but fails.*)

Fidget. Pshaw! You went and swelled dest as I dumped!

Doctor. Swelled! Ha! Ha!

Stephen. Ha! Ha! Come, Fidget. All be ready now.

> "Where did you come from baby, dear ?
> Out of the everywhere into here.

(He repeats each verse and they sing it.)

> Where did you get your eyes so blue ?
> Out of the sky as I passed through.
>
> Where did you get that pretty tear ?
> I found it waiting when I got here.
>
> Where did you get that pearl'y ear?
> God spoke and it came out to hear.
>
> How did they all just come to you ?
> God thought about me and so I grew.

Stephen. Come, now. Your little prayer. It's bed time.

(*They kneel and clasp their hands.*)

Calvin. (*They repeat after him in phrases.* Our father, thou did'st make the world and everything in it. Thou dost love everything which thou hast made.

Doctor. (*Aside to Stephen.*) I swear that's beautiful. I wish I were father to all the little homeless brats in America.

Calvin. (*Continuing.*) Thou dost love little orphans and wilt care for them. We pray Thee make every rough heart gentle, every cold heart warm and every vile heart pure. Save every human being and gather them all to thine arms when life is over. Amen.

Fidget. And bess poor Teven and Dack.

Stephen. Ha! Ha! Ha! Poor Teven and Dack! Dack is her little dog, Jack. About as disreputable and friendless a cur as God ever made. Good night, now. Good night!

(*He kneels for them to kiss him.*) *They each one put their arms around his and Calvin's neck and then Exeunt*)

Doctor. (*Aside.*) He may be guilty, but I swear it is hard to believe or suspect it.

Stephen. (*Aside.*) Poor Teven and Dack! Lone miserable dogs we are, too, Jack. We are fit companions, old fellow. Only you have no guilt on your head. (*Enter Martha with newspaper in hand.*)

Martha. Stephen, where is Philip? What do you think? His Susanna is dead.

Phil What's that Martha?

Martha. Oh, I beg your pardon, Philip. I—I Nothing. Nothing.

Phil. I heard you, Martha. I felt it. I knew it! Let me see the paper. (*He reads it to himself, drops the paper from his hands, gazes in quiet grief at the floor, draws a deep sigh and takes his seat. Martha watches his features closely; after a long pause, Philip is conscious of her eyes.*)

Phil. (*Very tenderly*) Is there anything I can do for you, Martha?

Martha. (*Aside.*) Pshaw! (*Turns and goes to Stephen.*)

Phil. (*Aside.*) That's a strange girl.

Doctor. Calvin?

Calvin. Yes.

Doctor. Do you know what I think of Stephen's trouble?

Calvin. Yes.

Doctor. You do? What?

Calvin. That he took the Midland bonds from the Treasury!

Doctor. Then, you are of the same opinion.

Calvin. I must say, I have entertained the suspicion, as dark and unwelcome a visitor as it may be, and yet, it is hard to think a heart so generous, so noble—

Doctor. You know his propensity to gambling?

Calvin. Yes. And you know how desperately he fights against it.

Doctor. True. I pity him with all my heart, but I'm going to question him. You watch him closely and Martha, too.

Calvin. My God! man You don't suspect her !

Doctor. Yes.

Martha. (*To Stephen.*) Be strong now. These people suspect us. I have felt their eyes. (*Going.*)

Doctor. Don't go yet, if you please, Miss Martha.

Martha. Certainly. (*Aside.*) The examination begins.

Doctor. Stephen, I have been thinking a great deal lately about the Midland bonds.

Stephen. So have I. Not only recently, but ever since they were taken.

Doctor. You know I don't believe that Withers did it.

Stephen. Indeed ! Why ?

Doctor. He left his trunk to be sent to the Inn. Beside, we know now that he intended to marry Rachel.

Stephen. Yes.

Doctor. And then his return to the scene of the crime—

Stephen. That very often happens. In fact it is a strange desire on the part of almost every criminal.

Doctor. The night of the robbery, did you see no one coming from the office ?

Stephen. No.

Doctor. Who was the next person you met after leaving the office ? I mean, after you first closed the vault ?

Stephen. Martha.

Calvin. Indeed.

Martha. Yes. I remember it perfectly. For old Mrs. Cody had worried and vexed me egregiously in the delay of finishing a basque for a dress which I was to wear that night. She promised to send it by five o'clock promptly and at seven, I went for it myself. You remember, Stephen how I hid myself behind the old well house and scared you as you came along? Ha! Ha !

Stephen. (*He whistles in a low key in apparently ab-stracted manner during the whole of Martha's speech.*) Yes.

Doctor. (*To Martha.*) And you saw no one come from the Treasury?

Martha. No, I couldn't see the Treasury at all.

Doctor. What did Stephen say when you scared him at the well?

Martha. Why he wasn't scared a bit. He said "Hel-lo, Martha, is that you? Where have you been?" And I told him. (*Aside.*) Calvin says nothing. I be-lieve he loves me. This Doctor suspects me and I'll be revenged on him if—

Calvin. Stephen! (*Stephen continues whistling.*) Ste-phen.

Stephen. Yes? What is it?

Calvin. Why do you pay such loose attention to this matter? You sit there whistling and looking as if your thoughts were in the planet Uranus. Have you no interest in this matter?

Stephem. Why, Calvin, of course I have. I have thought about it night and day ever since the night of the robbery. I am, myself, inclined strongly in the belief that Withers was innocent. When we reach home, I will employ the detectives again to ferret the matter out.

Calvin. (*To Doctor.*) I don't see any guilt there, Matt.

Doctor. Nor I either. Yet, there is something on his mind that is surely driving him mad.

Martha. (*To Stephen*) Why man you acted consum-mately. No actor could have done better. (*Aside.*) Suspect me? The sheep's heads. I'll teach them a lesson about meddling where they have no business. I must win Calvin if it's the last thing I ever do. Ha! That was a queer little pain went through me then. It was like an electric current. (*Pause.*) Pshaw! (*Exit.*) (*Enter at back Aunt Martha and Glenn.*)

Stephen. They now think me innocent. They can never prove our guilt. The secret is buried. That is, It's corpse is buried. It's soul, like an evil bird, cir-cles about my head unceasingly forever. (*Sighs.*) I told them the truth, and yet, it was a scalding, blist-ering lie! Ah. how different I am from the happy boy

that stood before the old Treasury and— There! I
do hope that walking will not return again. Yes, yes.
There it is again. I cannot stand it. I will not. I
will not endure it again. Doctor! Calvin! Glenn!
Aunt Martha! All!

Doctor. Another spell. Get me a little water. No.
Never mind. Take this, Stephen.

Stephen. (*Shaking convulsively.*) No, thank you.
Doctor, I deceived you. The Midland bonds. I did
not take them, but I was party to the crime. I, your
honored Mayor. Withers knew nothing of it, and
had nothing whatever to do with it. I tried to save
his life, but I couldn't do it. I knew Glenn was innocent, but was not brave enough to say so. When I
get back home, I will work my fingers to the bone for
her. The money from the sale of the bonds is all
gone. (*Pause.*) May I rest now? (*He breathes heavily
and grows more and more stupid.*)

Calvin. Can it be true?

Doctor. Well, well, well!

Glenn. Poor fellow, how I pity him. Oh, I could
endure the bitterest poverty all my life rather than the
knowledge that Stephen could be guilty of such a
crime. (*She sinks back into a chair, Calvin standing by
her.*)

Calvin. He has had a most terrific temptation to
endure, Glenn.

Glenn. Yes, yes. I know, I know. God pity him!

Stephen. Ah! What a load it has lifted off. (*Pause.*)
Oh, Captain! Have you any live stock on the vessel?

Captain. Live stock? Only a few sheep. That's
all.

Stephen. Sheep! It couldn't have been sheep I
heard last night. I heard — for I was as wide awake
as ever I was in my life—the sound of a horses' hoofs
standing and stamping impatiently on a stony road.
I reasoned with myself. I said I knew there was no
stony road, or any other kind of road, within 100
miles of the vessel. I thought that perhaps I had
been dreaming of taking a voyage to Australia, and
was not on board a ship at all. I got up, went to the
door, opened it, looked out and there were the great
waves, rolling beneath me and as far as I could see.
There! Upon my soul, I see it! as plainly as I see

my hand. A white horse, sauntering along over the
face of the sea. Bah! How can it be? And yet, I
see it. Oh, Pshaw! Pshaw! I swear I don't understand my condition. Calvin?

Calvin. Yes, Stephen.

Stephen. Look where I point.

Calvin. I do.

Stephen. Do you see anything?

Calvin. No. Nothing but the ocean and the sky.
What do you see?

Stephen. The ocean and the sky. (*Aside.*) It is
very strange.

(*First Gambler and Goozle heard quarreling without.*)

Goozle (*Without.*) Ha! Liar! It's mine.

1st Gam. (*Without.*) You are a liar, it's mine.

Goozle. It's mine, I say.

1st Gam. Let go, damn you, I'll kill you.

Goozle. Look out! (*Two shots fired in rapid succes-
sion. Exeunt Stephen and all the men, except Calvin.*)

Glenn. Stay here with us, Calvin.

Aunt M. Oh, horrible! How can they expect anything else than just such termination. How terrible
it is to die without hope, to be lost, eternally lost!
(*Re-enter Stephen and others.*)

Stephen. (*To Calvin.*) They threw his body in the
sea.

Aunt M. What's the matter Stephen?

Stephen. (*Pause.*) Aunt Martha— (*Aside.*) How
can I do it?

Aunt M. Did you know him, Stephen?

Stephen. Yes, Aunt Martha.

Aunt Martha. What was his name?

Stephen. Aunt Martha—I—have—very—heavy—
news for you, Aunt Martha.

Aunt M. For me, Stephen? Why, what can the
boy mean?

Stephen. Oh, be strong, Aunt Martha? Strong as
you never were, before?

Aunt M. For mercy's sake, Stephen. What? what?
what?

Stephen. That poor fellow was—

Aunt M. Who? who?

Stephen. Your own son!

Aunt M. Oh, my God! Stephen, what can you mean? My son! my son! My Richmond. He is safe at school, Stephen! Oh! Stephen, are you sure? Oh! Oh! Oh! my boy, my own precious boy! Oh, Stephen, are you not mistaken? Say you are Stephen,

Stephen. I wish to God I could, Aunt Martha.

Aunt M. Let me lie down here, Stephen. Let me lie here. Unbutton my dress, please, Glenn, and hold my hand close too, will you Glenn? I want to feel the blessed human touch. I never knew before how sweet it was! (*Captain passes through, followed by two officers.*)

Captain. Who did that shooting, Mr. Venable? (*Stephen points towards R.*) *Exit Captain and officers.*)

Goozle. (*Without!*) He drawed his iron fust, dideny boys?

Boys. (*Without.*) Yes, yes, yes. He did.

Goozle. (*Entering with Captain and soldiers.*) And shot first too, dideny boys?

Stephen. May I speak to him, Captain?

Captain. Certainly, Mr. Venable.

Goozle. Do yer think I'm goin to stand up and be robbed—

Stephen. Listen to me!

Goozle. And stole from and peppered wi' bullets too and not—

Stephen. Listen to me!

Goozle. Watcher want? (hic.)

Stephen. (Quietly.) There is the mother of the poor fellow you have just killed. (*Goozle staggers with drunken surprise, feels nervously about his clothes, slowly takes off his greasy cap, bows his head, stands thoughtfully, then goes slowly down on his knees, weeping. (Enter Ned Boyer, the mate.*

Ned. (*In hurried whisper.*) One moment, Captain. (*Exit Ned and Captain.*) *Goozle stands awkwardly about, not knowing what to do.*

Goozle. (*Beckoning Stephen to him.*) Your name's Shteben, ain't it?

Stephen. Yes.

Goozle. You won some dust fo' me, didenyer?

Stephen. Yes.

Goozle. Dair it is. Give it to her please. And—and Shteben! Pleash tell her dat I neber had no mother whut would own me fer her child! (*weeps.*) Will yer Shteben?

Stephen. Yes, I will. (*Listening.*) What noise is that below? (*Captain is heard running rapidly from below. He staggers in pale and almost fainting.*) What's the matter Captain?

Calvin. What's the matter, man?

Doctor. Speak, Captain, are you sick?

Captain. God help us! The vessel—is—sinking! The—the—read. (*handing paper to Doctor.*)

Doctor. (*Reading.*) "Capt. L. E. Cole, The Seagull is seaworthy. She will be ready for you next trip. Respectfully, A. L. Seymour, Commander." Why I see nothing in this, if the ship is seaworthy.

Captain. Oh! Oh! but—you—see—he—plainly meant—to—say— the Seagull is *not* seaworthy! for he says she will be ready for the *next* trip, meaning the one *after this!*

Doctor Can't you repair it? (*They begin to take off their coats.*)

Captain. No. Impossible! It is leaking slowly all around. The timbers are old and rotten.

Calvin. Then the life-boats, are they sufficient?

Captain. They—have—been—washed—away! Oh! God! pity my poor wife and little children! (*Falls on his knees.*)

Calvin. Then what are we to do, Captain?

Captain We must die my friend.

Glenn. Oh. Calvin? (*She throws her arms tight around him.*)

Calvin. "Thy will be done!" (*They tremblingly huddle together like sheep in a snow storm; Stephen extends his hand to Philip who takes it warmly; Calvin and Doctor stand and look into each other's faces and then grasp hands like faithful comrades that are not afraid to meet certain death; Stephen offers his hand to them. They take it. Glenn comes forward barely supporting herself and falls on Stephen's breast; he pauses as she approaches, gives her a look of bitterest sorrow and self-reproach and then receives her in his arms; turns his face away and weeps; then the gamblers learn the fact and look at each other in fearful consternation; one of them puts down a glass of beer which he was in the act of drinking. One of them converses rapidly in dumb show with others, pointing to Calvin; then one nervously takes a glass, pours water in it and beckons to Calvin, who approaches. Then extending the glass to him, Calvin refuses it, not understanding him; Gambler points to his head and to the others Calvin then understands and baptizes the three. Ceremony finished, they fall in agony on the floor—two on their knees and faces, the third between them on his back, his hands covering his face. The other two, without looking begin to feel with their hands for their comrades. Each takes a hand of the third. During all this solemn pantomime of silent despair, is played softly Beethoven's Moonlight Sonata First Movement.)*

Stephen. Calvin!

Calvin. Yes, Stephen.

Stephen. The little children! Can nothing be done for them? (*Calvin shakes his head sorrowfully.*) And they must drown too? I will go and kiss their little feet. Oh! oh! oh! The only hallowed spot in this vile, wicked heart;—my love for little children? And they must drown, too! Thank God, they are orphans! No one will weep much for them except the old blind woman to whose old ears their happy voices were such sweet music!

Captain. Ned, run up and tell the old pilot to come down.

Aunt M. Oh, Calvin, perhaps he may wish to be baptized. Tell him, please, will you?

Ned. I will, Aunt Martha. (*Exit Ned, running.*)

Aunt M. Oh, Stephen, do you believe there is a wretch in all God's creation sunk so low that Heaven's pity cannot reach him?

Stephen. Not one, Aunt Martha, not one! God made us all and He knows how to take care of us in the last trying hour. (*Doctor goes out and returns with Fidget asleep in his arms.*) (*Re-enter Ned.*)

Ned. He will not come, Captain.

Captain. But did you tell him we must sink!

Ned. Yes, sir.

Aunt M. And did you ask him to be baptized?

Ned. Yes, Aunt Martha. He said the old wheel

had furnished him a living for 16 years, and he would
not desert it now.

Calvin. Oh, brave old fellow. He has a friend
there in the darkness with him somewhere. (*Pause.*)
Little Fidget! Oh, pity, pity, pity! (*Pause.*) Matt!

Doctor. What, Calvin?

Calvin. You believe now, don't you?

Doctor. (*Very calmly.*) Believe what, Calvin?

Calvin. In the wonderful love of God and in the
life beyond the tomb.

Doctor. Oh, I don't know, Calvin. I don't know
anything about that. (*Pause.*) But I would like to
be with you old fellow. I would like to be with you
always.

Calvin. (*Deeply moved*) You shall! You shall be
with me!

Doctor. If it be true, my boy, as you believe, I ask
nothing better than this little flower as a peace offer-
ing before the throne of God!

(*Enter Martha Delmar arrayed as Cleopatra.*)

Martha. Now for my last great victory. Of all the
men I ever knew, this Calvin is the most immovable.
And strangest of all, I feel a certain burning desire
to possess him entirely. He draws me to him. I
would never be satisfied without his presence. Can
it be that Martha Delmar is in love? Bah! I'll not
believe it. Ah, there he is. Ha! Ha! Don't be horrified, Mr. Parson. To the pure all things are pure.
It is Art, man, Art! Observe the delicate curving of
these limbs, the lithe movements of the body, the
poise of the head, the swelling of my heart—an ideal
Cleopatra, man, do you—

Calvin. Woman, prepare to meet your God.

Martha. (*Looking sanctimoniously upward.*) Oh,
dear. Ha! Ha! Sixty years hence!

Calvin. Now. You have only fifteen minutes to
live.

Martha. Do you mean to kill me?

Calvin. No.

Martha. Does anyone else?

Calvin. No.

Martha. Then how, why!

Calvin. The vessel is sinking.

Martha. Now you are trying to frighten me. Ha!

Ha! Ha! You mischievous fellow! Yet, why do
they all look so serious? They are pale, too. Why
do they kneel yonder? Captain, what are they
kneeling yonder for?

Capt. They are praying, woman.

Martha. Woman! I never saw such a floating
prayer-meeting before—

Capt. Look at me, Miss Delmar. This vessel is
sinking rapidly.

Martha. S—Sinking? And the life boats are sufficient?

Capt. They have been washed away.

Martha. Washed away! Then what will you do?

Capt. Die.

Martha. Oh, Captain, you do not mean it?

Capt. I swear, before God, it is true.

Martha. Die? Die, did he say? Glenn, lend me
your cloak. Let me have your shawl, please. I must
hide my naked body. Glenn, I have wronged you.
It was I that took the bonds. Yes I. It was I that
drove Masterson and Lundy and a host of others to
their graves. It was I that ruined Stephen. O, I
cannot ask for pardon. I am *too* guilty, too guilty
Is it really sinking rapidly? Oh, Calvin, I meant to
ruin you, too, but I loved you! I loved you! And I
must drown? (*She grows more and more frantic.*) And
I must die? Die? Die? Hereafter when there is any
hidden guilt on earth, say Martha Delmar did it! I!
Oh, could I but send a message to the shore!

Phil. You can do it, Martha.

Martha. How? How?

Phil. In a bottle. Get a bottle quick, Ned.

Ned. Here's one.

Phil. Now Martha, write.

Martha. Oh, I cannot write. You do it, Philip.
And write as you never wrote before! Write for your
very life, good Philip.

Phil. My life! About the most worthless thing in
my possession now, my Martha.

Martha. Then for the sake of your immortal soul;
for the sake of your lost love, Susanna— .

Phil. Ah! I will write! Thank God, I shall soon
be with her again. (*Writing rapidly.*)

Martha. Almighty God, keep together the fast-breaking pieces of my mind until I can perform this last act.

Phil. (*Reading.*) "At sea, on board ship Sea Gull, July 10th, 1850. Know all men by these presents that I, Martha Delmar, do hereby"—

Martha. (*Dictat ng*)—solemnly swear in the presence of death and Almighty God that it was I that took the Midland Bonds, I that ruined Stephen Venable; I that set the sheriff after poor little Rachel's sweetheart and murdered him; I that set fire to Philip's trunk—

Phil. (*Looks up in surprise. Still writing and repeating the words as he writes.*) "For which he forgives me with all his heart." All right, go ahead.

Martha. I that did everything mean and wicked and cannot find it in my heart to ask forgiveness. That's all.

Calvin. (*Approaching her.*) Martha?

Martha. Don't touch *me!* Not *me!* "Unclean! Unclean!" Let me sign, good Philip, quickly. (*She writes her name desperately and sinks back in chair.*)

Aunt Martha. Write something for me Philip, just a little, to poor little Rachel. Tell her if she ever sees any poor wistful creature passing, to stop him and feed him and say *I* beg his pardon. And may God love her and wrap her close in his arms forever more.

(*Philip folds papers rapidly and places them in bottle and seals it.*)

Phil. Messages from eternity! (*Swinging the bottle out into the waves.*)

Martha. Look! Do you see that? It is coming over the water. Oh, Stephen, do you think it will climb over the rail?

Stephen. What, Martha?

Martha. See there! It is climbing over and it is the very one I fed with Rachel's mocking bird! Kill it! Kill it! Why don't you kill it? Keep it off, off. Don't le. it wind about me! Help! Help! Why do you stand there gazing at me! It has fastened my legs! It is wrapping my arms! Quick! Quick! Help! Help! (*Screams and appears to see serpent with head erect looking her in the face. After horrible pause, she slow-*

ly moves an arm, then appears to take the serpent by the neck and slowly unwraps it from her form. She then imagines it on the floor, coiled and ready to strike. She screams, turns, throws her hands over her ears, runs wildly and blindly about, then screams and jumps over the rail into the sea.)

Calvin. (*Calmly.*) Alas, poor wretch! May her miserable tortured spirit soon find its peace within the bosom of the Eternal Pity.

(*A great noise of water is heard below.*)

Capt. We're lost! The water is on the lower deck! We're lost! Oh, merciful God! (*They fall on their knees and faces.*)

Stephen. Listen! Oh, listen! Don't you hear that music? Don't you hear it? Ah, sing on, old Treasurer! We are coming to you!

(*The vessel sinks and the sea rolls over it.*)

CURTAIN.